I0752669

THE ETERNAL FLAME

Written by Israel Cazares II

Illustrated by Kumuditha Herath

ISBN 979-8-218-24067-7

To Malachi

Table of Contents

Prologue

Perhaps you've heard of the legendary Eternal Flame. You may have heard rumors about the man who could touch fire without injuring himself, or maybe you've even seen a glimpse of a flaming man soaring through the air during the dark midnight hours. Perhaps you've seen him in a dream, fighting to protect the great planet of Valor, Regardless, I can assure you, The Eternal Flame is real, and I fought by his side once upon a time. He was indeed what many would call a true hero, and I believe that his story is worth telling. He made many sacrifices in his life, sacrifices that I am alive today because of. So, I suggest that you take a seat, bundle up nicely, and enjoy the legend of The Eternal Flame.

- Sincerely, Johnathan Everett Gold

Prologue

The edge of the universe expands faster than the speed of light. Because of this, it's always covered in darkness. The darkness of the north edge of the universe is home to the greatest evil ever imaginable. The wicked emperor Lord Vencrim built his castle there. Vencrim spent most of his prolonged life conquering planets to expand his universal empire. He did so with his massive robot army, which he built himself after decades of study and experiments. He built mechanical foot soldiers, pilots, guards, and assassins. Dozens of planets had already fallen to Lord Vencrim and his metal army.

Of all his creations, Lord Vencrim was most proud of Lord Leveena, his unique assassin robot. Today, Leveena was tasked with retrieving an old scroll that was guarded by a clan of trolls on the planet Lak Ekliese. The trolls were said to be fearsome and mighty, but Leveena was the greatest killer in the universe. If she wanted that scroll, then nothing would stop her from getting it.

A loud knock echoed through the dark throne room of Lord Vencrim's castle. Vencrim waved a hand toward his sentinel robots, who opened the enormous metal doors. A dark hooded figure entered the room. She held a long dagger in her right hand that was covered in green blood.

"I assume that your mission was a success," Lord Vencrim said in a dark malevolent voice.

Leveena looked up at Vencrim to reveal two robotic eyes that glowed with a purple color.

"Of course it was, Master," Leveena replied as she wiped a few drops of troll blood off her silver skin. "Those dumb animals never stood a chance."

Leveena snapped her fingers. Two tall robots with purple eyes walked into the throne room carrying an old wooden chest. These were assassin robots, just like Leveena. However, they were not nearly as advanced. Leveena's eyes were as detailed as a human's, only every major part was a different shade of glowing purple. The other robots had eyes that were merely glowing orbs. Leveena's advanced robotic body was the only thing keeping her from being a human. The other robots had no free will. They were just mindless androids.

Lord Vencrim rose from his throne and walked over to the chest. His heavy footsteps echoed through the throne room. Lord Vencrim opened the chest and found an old scroll, which nearly fell apart as he opened it. Vencrim sat back down as he read. Leveena wondered why this scroll was so important. Vencrim had been very eager to find it, and he made it very clear that the scroll was not to be destroyed. Vencrim sighed as he read. He now seemed troubled. This was unusual since nothing ever troubled Lord Vencrim. After a few moments of reading and rereading, Lord Vencrim stood up from his throne and handed the scroll to Leveena.

"Prepare your assassins immediately," Lord Vencrim commanded. "I will prepare my army"

"What for?" Leveena asked.

In a sudden fit of rage, Vencrim grabbed Leveena by the neck. He raised his free hand toward his giant morningstar mace, his powerful magic weapon. The mace flew to his hand as it glowed with an eerie blue-green light. This frightening weapon was the source of Vencrim's great evil power.

"Do not question me, girl!" Vencrim roared. "Be grateful that I even let you live to serve me!"

With that, he threw her to the floor. Leveena gasped as she hit the ground. She didn't need air to survive, but Vencrim could still have killed her at any moment.

"I'm sorry, Master," Leveena replied quickly. "My assassins will be ready immediately."

"Good," Vencrim responded. "See to it that they are. We have no room for error in this matter, Leveena. My life may depend on it."

Leveena bowed, then quickly left the throne room.

"I hope so," she said to herself.

Chapter One:
The Birth of a Legend

Matthew was surrounded by bright orange flames. Sweat poured down his face. The heat of the hotel lobby was unbearable. Matthew ducked down behind the main desk, his back toward the kitchen. This was the safest place he could hide now. Matthew took another glance toward the kitchen. The gas tank would explode any second now. Matthew tightly hugged the crying baby in his arms. A tear rolled down Matthew's cheek.

"I'm sorry," he said.

Two hours earlier...

May 15, 2000

Matthew pushed his hand through the warm sand. He looked out toward the strong waves of the Pacific Ocean. The sound of the waves crashing into the rocks on the shore calmed Matthew as the hot sun warmed his body like a hot towel. Matthew watched a man and a woman as they walked along the beach together. In between them was a little boy, who smiled as they all walked together, holding hands as a happy family. Matthew imagined himself in that position, walking with his own family on the beach. Afterward, they might have ice cream together, and they would laugh. He would finally be happy. Matthew had never met his family, but for some reason, he still missed them. He missed them the most each year on this specific, spring day, his birthday. Matthew fought back the tears that slowly pushed their way toward his eyes. He didn't want to care about his family. He didn't want to have to live with the pain of never knowing them, but he did, and it hurt. It hurt so much.

A friendly hand fell on Matthew's shoulder. Matthew looked up to see his one true friend, a fellow orphan named Waldo. Waldo always knew that Matthew was hurting, but he never knew just what to say. Today all he could do was smile and say, "Happy birthday, Matt."

Matthew stood up and wiped a tear from his eye.

"Thanks, Waldo," Matthew replied as Waldo hugged him.

"I love you, Matt," Waldo said.

Waldo handed Matthew a gift-wrapped present. Matthew took the gift in his hands.

"You didn't have to do this," Matthew said.

Waldo waved Matthew off.

"I know," he said, "but I wanted to."

Matthew smiled as he tore open the wrapping paper to find an empty journal with a leather cover. Branded into the bottom corner of the cover were Matthew's initials, MB, for Matthew Benson. Matthew almost lost another tear.

"How much did it cost?" Matthew asked.

"Don't worry about it, Matt," Waldo answered. "It's your twelfth birthday. You should celebrate."

Matthew gave Waldo a big hug.

"Thank you, Waldo," Matthew said.

“Of course,” Waldo replied.

Matthew appreciated having at least one person he could call family.

• • •

Matthew and Waldo walked through the city together. They lived in San Diego, California, where there were beaches, restaurants, and dozens of hotels. Matthew and Waldo both worked in the city as car and window washers. People were usually nice to the boys, but they were often looked down on as lesser people. Sometimes people even hit them out of anger when they were dissatisfied with their service. Today Matthew and Waldo had chosen not to work because of Matthew’s birthday. Waldo had gone out in the morning to buy the journal, while Matthew had gone to the beach to relax for a while. Because Waldo was celebrating with him today, Matthew was having the best birthday of his life. Usually, they would’ve taken a bus to get back home from the beach, but today they decided to take a long walk together instead. They walked through the big city with its tall skyscrapers to get back to their small home. On the way to the orphanage, Matthew noticed that something felt different today. Everything was covered in a strange orange color. A nearby scream pierced the air.

“Something’s wrong...” Matthew said.

Waldo looked up at the sky.

“Hey, look at that!” he said.

Matthew looked up. A huge pillar of smoke rose from behind several tall buildings

“Is that a fire?” Matthew asked Waldo.

“Let's go see,” Waldo replied.

Waldo and Mathew turned a few corners of the long city streets. The pillar of smoke appeared to grow larger as the boys ran toward it. After turning one last corner, Matthew found a tall hotel that was burning throughout the middle floors. Several fire trucks had parked around the building, and dozens of people stood outside to watch the fire. People were screaming, sirens were blaring, and the fire was blazing violently. Matthew watched as a woman was dragged out of the building. She was exhausted and covered in ashes. The woman was quietly muttering words to the firemen, but nobody was listening to her. The firefighters that held her propped her up against a firetruck and left her there. Waldo and Matthew ran over to her. Waldo got down on his knees and checked the woman's pulse. She was barely moving.

“Are you okay?” Waldo asked her.

The woman, still muttering, put her hand on her chest.

“Baby... my baby is there... on the top...”

With that, she passed out. Matthew and Waldo were silent for a minute. Waldo called for help.

“Hey!” he called. “Somebody’s still inside!”

The firefighter shook his head.

“It’s too late, kid. The building’s too unstable now. We’re not going back in.”

Matthew couldn't believe what he had just heard. A human being was left in that building to burn. Matthew looked at the woman. He noticed that in her shirt pocket was a room key for the hotel. That's why her hand was on her chest. Matthew thought about his own family. He didn’t know who they were, but he knew that he would die to save them if he could. This woman still had her family, and Matthew wouldn't let it die today. Matthew put his journal on the ground as he slowly grabbed the key. He stared at it for a moment before taking one last glance at Waldo, who already knew what Matthew was going to do.

"Don't..." Waldo started.

But it was too late; Matthew was already running toward the building at full speed.

• • •

All was well inside the lobby. It seemed that the fire was only burning in the center of the building. Matthew found the stairs and ran up as fast as he could. Matthew could feel the heat once he reached the sixth floor. He was close to the fire now. Once he reached the seventh floor, he saw the fire through the glass window of the door to the nearby hallway. The heat was intense, and the flames were huge and bright. It was like he was looking through an oven window. Matthew continued running until he reached the top floor. He looked back at his card key. Room 1109. Out of breath, Matthew walked over to the door and unlocked it with the card. He opened the door and walked inside the room. He could hear someone crying. Matthew walked over to a small crib and found a tiny baby wrapped in a blanket. Matthew had been expecting a toddler, so the sight of a helpless baby caught him off guard for a moment. This was a tiny newborn girl, with small strips of blonde hair. Matthew picked up the bundled baby and began to leave.

"I've got you," he said to her.

Matthew began his descent to the lobby. On the ninth floor, Matthew was met with clouds of smoke, which burned his eyes. Matthew took off his button-up shirt and placed it carefully over the baby's head out of fear that she would suffocate on the smoke. On the eighth floor, Matthew was met with fire. He found a pile of burning wooden bars in the middle of the stairs. He tried his best to move around them, but he burned himself on the stair railing. Matthew carefully put down the baby and began to lift the burning wood. Matthew cried out in pain as he burned his hands. Lifting with all his strength, Matthew tossed the wood out of the way. Out of breath, Matthew looked down at his hands, which were already blistered. Matthew picked up the baby and continued down the stairs. After a few minutes of carefully avoiding random pieces of debris on the stairs, Matthew reached the bottom floor. The lobby had already caught fire. Everything was burning. Matthew raced toward the main exit. He could see the lights from the fire trucks outside. It looked like he was actually going to make it. A second before he could feel the fresh air from outside, Matthew was blocked by large metal beams that fell from the ceiling, creating a huge pile of debris in front of the exit. Matthew felt a wave of fear as he searched for another exit. He was running out of hope. Matthew turned toward the kitchen. Maybe there was a back door there. As he walked into the kitchen, Matthew did spot a back door. He tried to open it, but it wouldn't move. Debris must have blocked it from the outside. Beginning to worry, Matthew turned away from the door. He saw a large gas tank that had already been covered by fire. The metal was starting to heat up. It wouldn't be long before it exploded. Matthew panicked and ran back into the lobby. This was it. There were no more exits. Matthew was surrounded by bright orange flames. Sweat poured down his face. The heat of the hotel lobby was unbearable. Matthew ducked down behind the main desk, his back toward the kitchen. This was the safest place he could hide now. Matthew took another glance toward the kitchen. The gas tank would explode any second now. Matthew tightly hugged the crying baby in his arms. A tear rolled down Matthew's cheek.

"I'm sorry," he said.

A huge explosion came from the kitchen, destroying everything in the nearby area. Matthew was hit by the fire, which covered him in seconds.

Outside, the explosion was both seen and heard. The people gasped as large flames poured out of the hotel windows, momentarily taking the shape of a fire-breathing dragon, which roared once, then quickly disappeared. This strange incident was forgotten as the hotel collapsed in on itself, dropping thousands of pounds of debris on top of Matthew. The people outside were shocked. They had seen the boy run in, but he had never come back out.

Inside, a little baby girl was crying. She was mostly unharmed, but the person who protected her with his back to the fire was gone. His back had burned black, and he had died in seconds. Outside, Waldo was down on his knees with Matthew's journal in hand, crying for his lost brother.

• • •

Matthew saw a beautiful castle. It was tall and white, with a light-blue roof. Inside, the castle was filled with treasures, and the ceilings were made of silver and gold. The castle faded away as Matthew saw a man that stood nearly eight feet tall. He looked like a giant robot, and he had a sinister expression of hatred on his cold face. Matthew saw a man in a green suit of armor. The man flipped around like an acrobat, and he swung two short swords at Matthew. Matthew then saw a girl, maybe only a few years older than him. This girl was a robot, and she tried to kill Matthew. Her purple eyes glowed from underneath her black hood, and her sharp sliver claws buzzed with electricity. She screamed in rage as she threw a bolt of purple lightning at Matthew.

Matthew woke up with a gasp. His eyes, which were fully white a moment ago, began to return to their normal colors. His burned back began to heal itself, and after a few moments, it was back to normal, fully restored. Matthew found that the baby was asleep, but she was okay. She only had a small burn mark over her left eye down to her lip. Matthew was alive, and he felt stronger than he did before the fire.

"How am I alive?" he asked himself.

He wondered how he could have possibly survived the explosion. Matthew tried to stand up. He tore off the burned remains of his plain white undershirt as he noticed that his body had changed; he was now physically stronger than he was before. He had larger arms and abs on his stomach. Now he felt powerful when he stood, like a tall athlete.

"What... happened to me?" he asked himself.

He was afraid. He should have been dead. Matthew studied his surroundings. It looked like he was inside a small cave in a massive pile of debris. Matthew tried to move a large beam, which he knew would be incredibly heavy. Matthew was surprised when he lifted it with relative ease. He continued to carefully move pieces of metal and wood until he could see the sky above him. He called out for help and several firefighters came over to help him. They moved away pieces of debris until they were able to pull Matthew and the baby out of the hole. Matthew handed the baby to her mother, who was waiting at the top of the hole.

"Thank you," she said as she hugged her baby.

Several reporters tried talking to Matthew, and dozens of cameras flashed in his face. Matthew was overwhelmed and afraid, so he ran away. He held on to his burned shorts as he quickly made his way back to the orphanage with incredible speed. Once he arrived at the orphanage, Matthew carefully opened the door. All the other kids were awake and at the dinner table, crying. Waldo was with them. He had just finished telling them that Matthew had died in a fire. When Matthew's younger brothers saw him, they immediately ran toward him and hugged him. Waldo hugged Matthew the tightest.

"I thought you died," Waldo cried.

"So did I," Matthew said.

• • •

Matthew finished telling Waldo all about what had happened. He had told him about his strange vision, the pile of debris, and his new strength. Of course, Waldo thought that Matthew was suffering from some kind of head injury.

"Are you sure you're okay?" Waldo asked.

"I'm fine," Matthew repeated as he put on his pajamas. "I don't know how this is possible, but it really did happen. Somehow, I'm alive, but I know I shouldn't be."

Matthew lay down on his bed. Waldo did the same.

"We'll talk more tomorrow," Matthew said.

Waldo nodded as he put his glasses next to the bedside lamp.

"Okay," Waldo said. "Happy birthday, Matt."

Matthew closed his eyes and fell asleep.

• • •

Hours later, in the middle of the night, a sleek purple jet flew down from the sky and hovered above the orphanage. The jet landed on the roof without making a sound. A metal platform opened up on the side of the jet as a girl walked out. She wore a futuristic armor suit and helmet, which was purple like her jet. She wore a long black cape, which complemented the thin black segments on her armor. The mysterious girl made her way down to the orphanage. She climbed down the fire escape and paused for a second as she looked through Matthew's window. The girl opened the window and carefully stepped inside. She found a small backpack and began to fill it with Matthew's clothes. She found a journal and pen and put them in the bag as well. The girl flung the pack on her back and pulled out a small gun. She activated the gun and fired it at Matthew. A small dart pierced Matthew's arm, injecting him with a serum that would keep him asleep for a while. The girl walked over to Matthew and looked at his face. He wasn't sleeping peacefully. Something was troubling him. The girl felt sorry for him. Little did she know that this was how he slept every single night. The girl picked up Matthew and carried him out the window. She climbed back up the fire escape and walked back into the jet. After strapping Matthew into the co-pilot seat, she prepared the jet for takeoff. The jet hummed softly as she powered it up. The girl pressed a button on the side of her helmet.

"I have The Eternal Flame," she said. "I'm returning to Valor now."

The girl flew the jet up into the sky. The ship quickly accelerated as the jet shot up into space.

"Here we go," she said to herself.

The girl flew the jet straight into the sky. Matthew woke up just in time to see millions of bright colors as the jet soared through outer space.

Chapter Two: Welcome to Valor

A tall man in black armor swung his giant mace at Matthew, who slipped and fell as he struggled to avoid it. The evil warrior wore no helmet. He was bald and he had a scar that cut down from his left eye down to his upper lip. He laughed at Matthew, taunting him.

"You will die tonight, boy!" he roared.

Matthew woke up hyperventilating just as the man crushed him with his mace. He sighed as he wiped the sweat away from his forehead. It was just a bad dream. A terrible nightmare. Matthew rubbed his eyes as he tried to look around. Now, instead of being surrounded by darkness, Matthew saw millions of bright lights through his tired eyes. Was this still a dream? Matthew tried to open his eyes wider. He was strapped into the seat of some type of vehicle, and it looked like it was moving fast. Matthew looked out of the front window of the vehicle, which covered most of his view. It looked like he was in some kind of cockpit. Matthew tried to focus on what was outside the windows, but he could barely see. It was like something was trying to keep him asleep. Matthew felt his face getting warmer. He stopped and took a deep breath. Matthew was confused, but he knew that he wasn't imagining what he was seeing. He watched as his arms began to glow red, like hot metal. The heat started at his hands and climbed up his arms toward his neck. The hot energy covered his face, cleansing his head. The heat burned the tranquilizer out of his body. Matthew opened his eyes, but now he couldn't believe what he saw. Dozens of large planets could be seen all around. Matthew was sitting in a jet flying millions of miles per hour through space. Hundreds of bright stars surrounded Matthew's view. Colorful nebulas covered the sky near the jet.

"I have to be dreaming," Matthew said to himself.

Matthew hadn't noticed the person sitting next to him, but they heard Matthew speak out loud. The person turned in their seat toward Matthew and they pointed a small gun at his chest. Matthew didn't have the chance to ask any questions about where he was or why he was there. He didn't even have a chance to look at the person, who shot him with the blaster. Matthew's eyes felt heavy again as he quickly drifted back to sleep.

• • •

Matthew opened his eyes. The tranquilizer had finally worn off. Instead of a jet, Matthew now found himself locked inside some kind of prison cell. The entire cell was made of stone, with only one window letting in a few beams of light. The room was damp, but also freezing cold. A thin layer of frost covered the walls of the room. Matthew's hands and feet were completely covered in metal, which had been welded onto the chair he sat on. A metal mask covered Matthew's entire head, clamping his mouth shut. Matthew quickly breathed in and out through his nose. He was scared. Some psychopath must have trapped him in this cell.

Matthew tried to calm down and think. Who would kidnap him? And why? Matthew tried to pull away from the restraints, but they wouldn't even move. He was stuck here. Disappointed, Matthew sighed through his nose. A puff of steam shot out from his face. The steam was hot, unnaturally hot. Matthew knew he hadn't been dreaming. Something strange did happen last night, and it affected him somehow. Matthew puffed another blow of steam. This time, the steam hit the wall, causing the frost to melt into water droplets. Matthew had an idea. If he could create enough water on his hands, he could use it to slip out of the shackles. Matthew aimed his nose toward his right arm and blew out a puff of steam. Matthew was surprised to find out that the hot steam didn't hurt him. Instead, it only felt warm. Matthew kept blowing steam, and his plan was beginning to work. Water began to cover his arm and slip down toward his wrist. Matthew pulled at the restraint as hard as he could. With one last puff of steam, Matthew's right hand finally slipped out of the shackle. Matthew sighed in relief. He then tried to take off his head guard. It was made partly of tough fabric, like leather, but it was mostly made of metal plates and bars. Matthew pulled as hard as he could until his head slipped out of the helmet. This time, Matthew smiled to himself. It felt good to be able to move his mouth again. Matthew looked down at the helmet. Tiny metal bars covered the mouthpiece. If Matthew bent one of the bars, he could use it to pick the other locks.

"Come on..." Matthew said as he lifted the helmet above his head.

Matthew slammed the helmet down onto the left shackle of the chair. Nothing happened at first, so Matthew hit harder. The metal bars began to bend, so Matthew continued to slam the helmet. He needed to escape, and soon. Who knew what these people would do to him? Matthew slammed the helmet on the chair one last time. The bar finally bent inwards and broke. Using the empty right arm restraint as an anchor, Matthew pulled the helmet until the bar bent outwards. Matthew then inserted the bar into the left keyhole. He twisted and turned the helmet until the lock clicked open. Both of his arms were free. As Matthew moved on to the legs, he was distracted by a loud noise. The huge cell doors were slowly beginning to open. Somebody was coming. Matthew quickened his pace. His legs were still locked, and the doors were opening. Matthew tried to hurry as he continued picking. The lock on Matthew's left leg opened. One more to go. The door was almost open. Matthew struggled to pick open the last lock. A moment later, two guards entered the room. The guards wore silver armor that was partially painted white, and they held large wooden shields with beautiful crests. The guards entered the room and looked at the metal chair. The boy was gone. All that was left was a damaged head restraint lying on the seat of the chair. The guards spoke in an alien language and turned to leave. Matthew stood behind them in the hallway. He lifted his hands toward them and cried out in attack. Giant waves of fire shot out from Matthew's hands, hitting the guard's shields. The force of the fire pushed the guards backward as they hit the metal chair and were knocked unconscious.

"Woah..." Matthew said as he looked down at his hands in surprise.

He had expected something to happen, but he didn't know what. He didn't understand his powers yet. Matthew glanced down at the guards. They weren't moving anymore, and

Matthew hoped that he hadn't killed them. An alarm began to blare inside the building, causing red lights to flash. Matthew began to run away from the cell. It was time to leave this place. As Matthew ran through the hallways, he looked at his surroundings. The walls were made of white polished stone, and the ceilings were made of silver and gold. The floors were made of smooth marble.

"I'm in a castle," Matthew said to himself as he ran.

Matthew turned a corner and found two more guards. He was nearly surrounded now. In a panic, Matthew opened and ran through the nearest door. This door led to the outside of the castle, where Matthew was met by a huge field of white snow. Matthew ran as fast as he could away from the castle. He ran until he was pretty far ahead of the guards. The cold air burned Matthew's skin. The only protection he had against the cold was his old pajamas: a plain black t-shirt and shorts. Matthew looked back to the castle. He couldn't see the guards anymore. Just as Matthew thought he was going to escape, he noticed a huge cliff right in front of him. Matthew stopped as fast as he could, barely stopping at the edge of the cliff. Hundreds of feet below stood dozens of tall sharp rocks. This was a dead end. Matthew breathed heavily. This was it. He would either die here or be captured by the guards. Matthew looked down at the rocks as he wondered what he should do. His feet burned in the ice-cold snow.

"Careful," a robotic voice said.

Matthew turned around to see a girl that wore shiny purple armor and a helmet that covered her entire head.

"It's farther down than it looks," she said.

The girl pressed a button on the side of her helmet. The purple helmet slowly collapsed into smaller pieces until her whole head was revealed. The girl had light-colored skin, and she wore a layer of red lipstick. Her jet-black hair fell past her shoulders as her helmet disappeared, and her ears were slightly pointed at the top, like an elf. She was the most beautiful girl Matthew had ever seen.

"Welcome to Valor," the girl said as she extended a hand toward Matthew. "I'm Victoria."

Matthew hesitated before taking her hand.

"It's okay," Victoria said with a soft smile. "I'm not going to hurt you."

Matthew slowly lifted his hand.

"I'm... Matthe-" he began.

He was interrupted as the ground beneath him suddenly crumbled, dropping him down to the rocks below. Victoria jumped forwards and caught Matthew's hand just before he fell out of reach. Matthew looked down to the rocks, then back up to Victoria. She was staring down at him wide-eyed as if she was afraid that he would die. Matthew stared into her eyes, and she stared into his. Victoria pulled Matthew up to the ground.

"Thank you," Matthew said, out of breath.

Victoria nodded.

"Listen, I know you probably have a lot of questions," she said, "but let's go back to the castle first. I'll tell you everything you want to know once we're inside."

Matthew looked back at the white castle. It had a light-blue roof, just like the one from his dream. Matthew really was on an alien planet. Did he really want to go back inside? Victoria extended her hand toward Matthew, who hesitantly accepted it.

"Okay," he said.

• • •

Matthew and Victoria walked down the halls of the old castle. Matthew admired all of the beautiful portraits that hung on the walls. There were great kings of Valor that went back centuries. Victoria and Matthew reached a large room at the end of the hallway that was closed off by two enormous metal doors. It took four guards to pull them open.

"This is the throne room," Victoria informed.

She led Matthew inside the huge room and brought him to a long wooden table.

"You can sit down right here," Victoria said. "I need to go. I'll return in a few minutes with the king of Valor. He wants to speak with you."

Matthew sat down at the table.

"Okay," he replied. "I'll be right here."

Victoria smiled and left the throne room. Matthew began to look around the room. He hadn't seen this room earlier when he was running. At the far end of the room were the enormous doors, which had several locks and barricades built into them. It was the only entrance and exit to this room. Above the table hung an enormous golden chandelier, which held at least forty burning candles. On the closer side of the room sat a large throne. It looked like it was made of white marble, and it had blue gemstones embedded into it. Most of the castle was white with blue outlines. Blue and white must have been the primary colors of Valor. Overall, it seemed pretty normal, at least for an alien castle.

Matthew's train of thought was broken as a man approached him with a pair of black boots that sat on a silver tray. Next to the boots sat a hot towel and a pair of socks. In his other hand, the man held a new set of clothes. The man wore a white robe with silver-colored sandals. He spoke something to Matthew in a language that Matthew didn't understand or even recognize, then he handed him the tray.

"Are these for me?" Matthew asked him.

The man replied in the alien language. Matthew pointed to his feet.

"Do I put them on?" he asked him.

The man set the tray down on the table and picked up the towel. He bent down and rubbed Matthew's feet with it, cleaning off the dirt. After that, the man dried Matthew's feet with his white robe and put the socks on him, then he put the boots on him. Matthew thanked the man, who bowed his head and walked away. Matthew wondered why he had been treated so nicely. He also wondered what language the man had just spoken. Was it from Earth or Valor? Victoria had spoken perfect English, but Matthew guessed that not everybody on Valor could. Matthew planned on asking Victoria about it later. Matthew stood to his feet as he put on the other clothes that the man had given him. He put on a pair of black pants and a long green jacket that reached down a bit past his waist. Matthew began to walk around as he tested out the boots. They were surprisingly comfortable, and they felt nice and warm. After taking several steps, Matthew heard a large creaking noise as the doors slowly began to open again. Matthew quickly sat back down, not sure if he should have stood up in the first place. He watched as several guards marched in, followed by an older man with a beard that was mostly white. Victoria walked in after the old man, followed by two more guards. Matthew knew immediately that the older man was the king of Valor. He had no crown, but he wore a long, white robe and a silver necklace. He had little hair on his head, and he had a pale wrinkly face. Instead of taking a seat on his throne, he took a seat at the table across from Matthew. Victoria sat down at the king's right. The king smiled and extended a hand toward Matthew.

"Hello. I am Finnian McCallaghan, the King of Valor," he said in a quiet, yet strong, voice.

He had a thick Irish accent, but Matthew could understand him perfectly. Matthew accepted his handshake.

"Matthew Benson," he replied.

The king chuckled.

"Oh, I know," he said, "it's wonderful to meet you."

Matthew wondered why the king of an alien planet seemed so excited to meet him.

"I assume you have already met my daughter, Princess Victoria?" Finnian asked Matthew.

Matthew turned to Victoria. He hadn't known that she was his daughter.

"Yeah, I did," Matthew replied to the king. "She's really nice."

King Finnian seemed pleased. There was a moment of silence as several men in white robes appeared with food on silver platters. They must have been servants. They set down a large bowl of chili in front of Matthew. The food smelled delicious, and Matthew was hungry. He was just about to take a bite before he decided that he should probably ask the king for permission. The king had already started eating. Victoria wasn't eating, but she noticed Matthew's hesitation and nodded her head, so he began to eat. The chili was the most amazing food Matthew had ever tasted. It had a hint of smokiness to it, and it had some kind of very strong cheese. The pieces of meat were soft and tender. The king noticed how much Matthew enjoyed it.

"Do you like the venison chili?" King Finnian asked him.

Venison? That was deer meat. Matthew momentarily lost his appetite since he had never tried deer before and wasn't used to it.

"It's delicious," Matthew replied as he took another bite. "Thank you."

It was too good for Matthew to really care about what animal he was eating. After they had finished, several servants came to take their bowls away. They offered Matthew a second bowl, but he refused it. Matthew had a lot of questions, and he needed answers. He began with the most important question.

"Your majesty…" he started, "why did you bring me here?"

The king wiped his mouth with a napkin and cleared his throat. He sighed a long, troubled sigh.

"Where do I begin?" he asked himself.

He seemed to think about something for a moment before speaking again.

"I will answer your question, but first allow me to give you a bit of a background," he finally said.

"A long time ago, there lived a boy named Kier Vencrim. He was raised in a small village on a faraway planet near the end of the universe. Even from his youth, this boy was filled with pure evil. He had been twisted and corrupted by an evil spirit, a dark mirrored version of the good wizard Majesto. Kier learned dark magic from the evil Majesto, and he learned how to use the power of evil to hurt others and to benefit only himself in his life. His village confronted him about his dark magic. In a fit of rage, he slaughtered them all, every last one of them. This act of great evil earned him a powerful weapon called The Mace of Evil. The mace was one of ten ultimately powerful weapons, known as Omega Weapons. With this weapon, he became nearly unstoppable. Vencrim used his powers to become a warlord, and he was dedicated to creating a universal empire for himself. The good wizard Majesto, armed with the powerful Wand of Magic, attempted to defeat Lord Vencrim. Majesto failed, and he nearly died battling Vencrim. Desperate to find a way to stop Lord Vencrim, Majesto gazed into the future to find what he needed to stop Vencrim. Indeed, he found hope. In the future, a Warrior of Fire, the wielder of The Fire Sword, would defeat the Warrior of Evil in their Final Battle. Majesto wrote his findings onto a scroll, which was kept hidden on another planet. We know that one day the powerful Warrior of Fire, known as The Eternal Flame, will defeat Lord Vencrim on Belora-Kon, the Planet of Death."

Matthew sat in awe and confusion. His mind tried to process the information he had just received. He knew what it meant for him, but he hoped he was wrong.

"What does this have to do with me?" he asked King Finnian.

The king asked Matthew several questions in reply.

"Have you mysteriously acquired strange abilities recently?" he asked.

"Yes, I have," Matthew sighed.

"When you sat amongst the flames of that building yesterday, did you see a dragon in the fire?"

Matthew shook his head.

"No, I didn't," he answered.

"Have you seen strange visions since the incident?"

Matthew nodded slowly. A shiver climbed up his spine.

"I saw Lord Vencrim." Matthew admitted, "and a robot girl with metal claws."

King Finnian and Victoria were silent for a second. They both looked surprised and afraid that the girl was mentioned.

"The girl was Lord Leveena," Victoria finally said. "She's Lord Vencrim's personal assassin. She's twisted and full of hate. Leveena has killed more people than you could count, but nobody has seen her in months, not since she built her own castle on Valor in the nearby mountains."

Matthew didn't know who he should be more afraid of, Leveena or Vencrim. The king began explaining again.

"Matthew, I believe that while you were saving the child in the fire yesterday, you were killed."

This wasn't very hard for Matthew to believe. He had wondered how he had survived in the first place.

"How did I come back to life?" Matthew asked King Finnian.

"It is an ability of The Eternal Flame," he answered. "You experienced a Renewal, where you die and come back to life stronger and more powerful than before. It is rumored that The Eternal Flame may have as many as ten lives."

Matthew nodded his head understandingly. The king continued, "We have several satellites taking videos of Earth.

Outside of the hotel, a large dragon momentarily emerged from the flames."

King Finnian tapped a small black orb that was embedded into the center of the table. A hologram appeared over the orb and began to play a video of the hotel. Sure enough, a large dragon made of fire flew out from the flames. King Finnian explained that The Eternal Flame could have one of several fire beasts to represent them, such as a phoenix, or in Matthew's case, a dragon. Matthew had a new question.

"What's the difference between The Warrior of Fire and The Eternal Flame?" he asked.

"The Eternal Flame is the name given to the Warrior of Fire that has the greatest potential to truly destroy evil once and for all," King Finnian answered. "You are not the first, but you may be the last. Regardless, the powers of both the Warrior of Fire and The Eternal Flame rest in your hands. It is an immense burden to carry."

Matthew began to take everything in. King Finnian believed that Matthew was The Eternal Flame, the one destined to defeat Lord Vencrim. Matthew wondered how he could beat somebody as powerful as Vencrim. Matthew shared his question with the king.

"How could I possibly stand a chance against Lord Vencrim?"

The king turned toward Victoria.

"Victoria will train you for battle for about three years," he answered. "The Final Battle is speculated to take place in a few years on Earth's Christmas Day. Aside from that, once you find The Fire Sword, the all-powerful weapon of The Warrior of Fire, you will become even more powerful."

The king paused.

"Hear me, Matthew… I know that this is impossible to ask of anyone, but… We desperately need your help. Lord Vencrim has named Valor next on his list of planets to conquer. He's kept us alive this long only to toy with us, but he will destroy us eventually. If you don't become The Eternal Flame, we will all perish by his mace. So, I ask you... will you help us?"

Matthew looked down at the table. He felt afraid. He would have to devote himself to a short life of training, always expecting battles and war, never truly knowing peace. Matthew knew deep down that the power he now had was strong, but would he master it in time? And what about Waldo? Matthew would have to leave him alone in California.

"I…" Matthew started. "I think I need some time to think about it."

The king nodded his head.

"Of course," he said. "A decision like this should not be taken lightly. Take as much time as you need."

Matthew thanked King Finnian.

"In the meantime," the king finished, "Victoria will show you around."

Victoria rose from her seat, and Matthew did the same. He thanked the king for the meal as he followed Victoria out of the throne room.

•••

Matthew and Victoria walked past huge ruins of what was once a large city. A few stone buildings stood, but most of them had been reduced to mere pieces of stone.

"What happened here?" Matthew asked.

"Vencrim," Victoria answered sadly. "He attacked Valor about a year ago, and he destroyed everything here. He murdered hundreds of people."

Matthew walked over to a dry fountain that had stopped flowing.

"How did he do this?" Matthew asked.

"Look up there," Victoria said as she pointed to the sky.

A small white circle was faintly visible in the sky above.

"Vencrim placed that wormhole there last year. He has a fleet of powerful ships that fire lasers and missiles, which came through the wormhole. He destroyed the entire city in only a few hours."

Victoria kicked a rock that sat on the road.

"There's not much left now," she said sadly.

Victoria led Matthew to a smaller village, which had a few dozen houses and several markets. The houses looked like old-fashioned cottages made of wood with straw roofs. The smell of roasted pig lingered in the air, and the sound of a blacksmith's hammer could be heard nearby. Several young children ran through the road, playing happily. Some people wore thick clothes and animal skins. Other people had fewer clothes, and they sat alone in the icy dirt. Matthew looked at Valor with wonder, amazement, and pity. This planet was amazing, but it was poor and dying. Victoria could tell what Matthew was thinking.

"Valor wasn't always like this," she said. "We used to be a strong people, and we had excellent agriculture and trade. Our cities were always visited by people from other planets who came to buy goods. We were on the verge of becoming a futuristic utopia. But then people from another planet came to us asking for help against Lord Vencrim. We sent them our best men, but Vencrim destroyed our armies. Then, since we helped his enemies, he attacked us multiple times. We have very few soldiers left."

Matthew looked over at a man who had only one arm. He wore a dirty breastplate of a Valorian soldier. Victoria turned to Matthew.

"I can't expect you to join us," Victoria said, "but if you did... we might actually stand a chance."

Matthew looked down at the ground.

"I'm afraid of him... Of Vencrim," Matthew said. "I've seen him in my dreams. He's strong and terrifying. I don't think I could stop him alone."

Victoria was silent for a moment.

"Neither do I," she replied, "but we could stop him together."

Matthew looked up at Victoria. He gazed into her dark brown eyes.

"I swear to you that no matter how far you go to fight Lord Vencrim, I will be right there with you, every step of the way," Victoria promised, "and if we die fighting for Valor, we die together."

Matthew nodded. He was moved by Victoria's words, but he tried not to let it show.

"Okay," he nodded.

A loud beeping noise interrupted the silence. Victoria lifted her left arm and looked at her left gauntlet, which had an electronic control panel installed into it. Victoria pressed a button on her gauntlet, which caused a hologram to appear over her arm. Several black spaceships flew out of Vencrim's wormhole. The ships flew toward a green forest, where they were met by other ships that came from the mountains. One jet stood out from the rest, a black jet with silver wings and a purple light emanating from the front. Victoria's face was filled with fear.

"What is it?" Matthew asked.

"It's Leveena..." Victoria said, "She's going to attack the castle!"

Victoria turned around and ran toward the castle. Matthew tried to keep up with her.

"When will she get there?!" he shouted as he ran.

Victoria shouted back, "She's already there!"

Chapter Three: Leveena

A huge explosion shook the ground near the castle. A giant black ship hovered in the air nearby. The triangular ship had launched a missile at the castle, causing a large part of a tower to collapse. Dozens of bricks clattered to the ground. Another ship stormed by with a loud screeching sound. This one was far smaller than the triangle ship, and it had long sharp blades between the wings and a purple ball of energy that floated in front of the cockpit. The energy pulsated until a huge bolt of purple lightning shot out of it, striking the castle and creating a huge crack in the wall near the main gate. The large triangle ship dropped several large black crates to the ground. The crates opened up and several robot soldiers marched out of them. The robots were tall and they had red glowing eyes. They lifted their blasters toward the castle and began firing dozens of red laser beams. The few Valorian soldiers that stood near the castle attacked the robots, but they were quickly overpowered and shot down. The robots used explosives to expand the crack in the wall, creating a large opening for them to enter the castle. It was at this time that Matthew and Victoria reached the castle. Victoria looked out at the destruction with fear.

"They'll kill my father," Victoria cried. "I need to go help him."

With that, Victoria ran toward the back of the castle. Matthew, unsure of what to do, eventually decided to follow Victoria. Once Victoria reached the back of the castle, she used her gauntlet to electronically unlock the steel door. Matthew followed her inside just before the door slammed itself shut.

"What are you doing?!" Victoria asked Matthew as she turned around.

Matthew stuttered as he tried to explain himself.

"If Leveena finds you, she'll kill you!" Victoria shouted in a whisper.

"I didn't know what else to do," Matthew said, "but maybe I could help you."

Victoria sighed as she looked down the hallway, then back at Matthew.

"Fine," Victoria decided, "you can come with me. But you need to do exactly as I say. Let's go."

Victoria ran down the hallway with Matthew close behind her. As they reached the throne room, they found that the huge doors had been blown open. Victoria told Matthew to stop as she scanned the area. Several robots stood near the entrance of the throne room. More robots were inside, and they stood around King Finnian, who was forced to wait on his throne. Matthew looked at Victoria, but he couldn't tell what she was feeling. Matthew thought that she must have been really scared.

"Let's go," Victoria said as she walked away from the throne room.

Matthew followed her to a secret door in the nearest wall that opened up to reveal a long dark hallway.

"Where does this lead?" Matthew whispered.

"Shh..." Victoria whispered back. "Look."

The hallway had reached an end. A small wooden door stood at the end. Matthew looked through a tiny slot in the door, which showed the throne room right in front of them. Now Victoria and Matthew were far closer to King Finnian.

"I'm going to ambush them," Victoria said as she placed her hand over an electronic panel.

Matthew nodded.

"Wait!" he whispered suddenly. "What's that noise?"

Victoria listened. A metallic clanging sound echoed lightly through the air.

"We're too late..." Victoria whispered in defeat.

Several tall robots entered the throne room. These robots were taller than the others, and they had purple eyes. Following them was a girl with a black hood and cape. She had long black hair and robotic eyes that were almost human, but glowed purple instead. The girl had a silver face that was smooth and human-like. She had metal hands and fingers that had short sharp claws, but they weren't like the claws that Matthew had seen in his dreams. Matthew was afraid, but he thought that she actually looked kind of pretty in her own way.

"Leveena," Victoria whispered to herself.

The metallic clanging ended as Leveena stopped walking. Inside the throne room, Finnian shouted at Leveena, "What do you want, Lord Leveena?"

Leveena laughed. She sounded young, like Victoria, and she only had a slight robotic tone to her voice.

"Good to see you too, Finnian," Leveena said with a smile.

The king was not amused.

"I have no time for your games," he said bravely.

Leveena placed a hand on her chest.

“Dear Finnian, I haven't come here to play,” she replied. “What I’ve come here for is important. You see, I heard you’ve recently stumbled upon something... something powerful enough to defeat Lord Vencrim himself. Or should I say... someone?”

A chill crawled up Matthew’s spine. She was here for him, not King Finnian.

“I don’t know what you’re talking about,” Finnian replied.

Leveena stopped smiling.

“The Eternal Flame,” she demanded, “where is he?”

Matthew felt the air grow colder.

“I don’t know,” Finnian replied firmly.

Leveena sighed.

“Tell me Finnian,” Leveena began, “how has Victoria been? I haven’t seen her in so long.”

Both Victoria and Finnian were completely silent, waiting to hear what Leveena would say next.

“I love Victoria,” Leveena said sarcastically. “She was always so heroic and majestic. Nothing would stop her from being a hero, not even me. Surely, she would have stormed in here to protect you by now, unless... she was protecting someone more important than you.”

Leveena turned toward the wall as she lifted her left hand. Matthew heard a low humming noise as the hair on the back of his neck stood up. Small streams of purple lightning ran across Leveena’s fingers as the electric panel in the hidden hallway began to blink and glitch.

“Look out!” Victoria said as she pulled Matthew away from the wall.

Leveena's powers unlocked the secret door, opening it at her will. Matthew and Victoria's faces were filled with fear as they looked at Leveena face-to-face.

"There you are," Leveena smirked.

"Run!" Victoria shouted.

Matthew and Victoria ran back through the secret hallway. The robots in the throne room began firing at them.

"We need to get out of here now!" Victoria said as they ran back into the main hallway.

Matthew was terrified and out of breath.

"What do we do?" he asked Victoria.

Victoria looked down the hallway.

"We need to get to my jet," she replied quickly. "Let's go!"

Matthew followed Victoria toward the end of the hallway, where several large prison cells sat. These cells were new and futuristic, unlike the cell Matthew woke up in. A sharp sound caused Matthew and Victoria to turn around. Leveena stood behind them at the other end of the hallway. She used her metal claws to scratch the stone walls, creating bright sparks and a sharp scratching noise. Her eyes glowed from underneath her hood.

"You can't escape me," Leveena taunted as she pulled out two long daggers from her belt.

Victoria's helmet rebuilt itself around Victoria's head.

"Watch me," Victoria said in a robotic voice.

Leveena and Victoria ran toward each other. Leveena swung her dagger at Victoria, who blocked it with her right gauntlet. Victoria tried to punch Leveena with her left hand, but Leveena used her claws to quickly slash from Victoria's left shoulder across to her chest. Leveena's claws cut through Victoria's armor, but they didn't reach her skin. Victoria pushed Leveena away, and they stared at each other for a moment.

"Your move," Leveena taunted.

Matthew noticed that the soles of Victoria's metal boots began to glow. Victoria cried out as she used rocket boots to fly forward and grab Leveena. Victoria pushed Leveena up to the ceiling and smashed her into it. Victoria let Leveena fall back to the ground. As Leveena hit the ground, she lifted her hand and used her powers to make Victoria's suit malfunction. The jet boots stopped working and Victoria fell to the ground. Matthew stood behind Victoria. Leveena stood on the opposite side of Victoria.

"Run, Matthew!" Victoria yelled.

Matthew didn't move. Leveena laughed as she walked over to Victoria, who was still lying on the ground. Leveena raised her dagger.

"Goodbye, Victoria," Leveena said.

Matthew lifted his arms and shouted, "Noo!!!"

As he lifted his arms, huge flames shot from Matthew's hands, hitting Leveena. Leveena raised her arms to block the flames, but she was forced back into one of the open cells. Matthew ran to the cell and pressed the biggest button on the panel, causing a wall of glass to cover the front of the cell. Leveena was trapped for now. As soon as the door was sealed, Victoria's suit powered back up. She stood up and walked over to Matthew.

"Thank you," Victoria said.

Matthew nodded as he turned to Leveena, who was laughing.

"I wasn't expecting that," Leveena said. "So... you're The Eternal Flame. You're cute."

Caught off guard, Matthew opened his mouth to speak as he turned to look at Victoria. He was visibly uncomfortable.

"Don't listen to her," Victoria said.

Matthew looked back at Leveena.

"My master sent me to kill you," Leveena said. "With Lord Vencrim, failure isn't an option. I hope you understand."

Matthew swallowed.

"We need to go," Victoria said to Matthew.

Leveena smiled.

"Please let me out," she said calmly. "I promise I won't hurt you."

Leveena menacingly dragged her sharp finger on the glass, scratching it with a sharp screech. Matthew began to back away from the cell.

"Okay, let's go," he said to Victoria.

Leveena waved her fingers as Matthew left.

"See ya soon," she taunted.

• • •

Victoria fought through a group of robots outside. They had begun to shoot at her, but Victoria's armor made her punches and kicks stronger, making quick work of the robots. Once she finally reached her jet, she powered it up. Matthew walked into the cockpit and sat down in the copilot seat. Another wall of the castle blew open as Leveena walked outside. She had several robots with her, who began to blast at Victoria's jet. Victoria immediately accelerated the jet at full speed, pushing Matthew back into his seat. The pressure felt intense as the jet quickly lifted off the ground.

"Hold on," Victoria said.

The jet shot straight up into the air. The sky turned from blue to black as the jet exited the atmosphere of Valor. Victoria waited a few minutes before stopping the jet in space. Valor looked like a tiny white and blue coin from up in space. Vencrim's wormhole had disappeared. Matthew figured it must have closed after the robots attacked. There were a few moments of silence before Victoria sighed. They had successfully escaped Valor.

"We made it," Victoria said.

Matthew sighed in relief.

"Wait," he started, "what about your father?"

Victoria shook her head.

"I don't know," she replied.

A light began to blink on the dashboard of the jet. Victoria pushed a few buttons as a hologram of Lord Leveena appeared over the dashboard.

"Hello, Victoria," Leveena said. "I think you forgot something."

The hologram showed King Finnian, who had already been beaten by several robots.

"I have your father alive, for now," Leveena continued, "but he won't stay that way. I'm giving you ten minutes to bring me The Eternal Flame. If not, your father dies."

Leveena laughed evilly.

"It's your choice," Leveena said as the hologram ended.

Victoria put her face in her hands as she began to quietly cry. Matthew sat helplessly in the co-pilot seat. Victoria would have to turn him over. Matthew knew that neither he nor Victoria could just let King Finnian die. Matthew would have to take his place.

"Let's go back," Matthew said to Victoria.

Victoria wiped a tear from her eye.

"We can't," Victoria said sadly. "I can't let you die, you're too important. You are prophesied to defeat Lord Vencrim. Besides, Leveena might still kill my father anyway."

Matthew sighed.

"Then what do we do?" he asked.

Victoria shook her head again.

"I don't know," she answered.

Matthew tried to think. How could they stop Leveena? He wasn't powerful enough but... what if he could be?

"What about the Fire Sword?" Matthew asked.

Victoria looked up at him.

"What about it?" she asked.

"If we found it, I would become even more powerful, right?" Matthew asked.

Victoria nodded her head.

"What if we offered it to Leveena? Since I need the sword's power to defeat Vencrim, she might accept it in my place."

Victoria sat in silence for a minute.

"It's worth a shot," she finally said. "We'll see if Leveena will accept it."

Victoria started a live hologram.

"Leveena," Victoria started, "I am coming to you with a proposal."

Leveena smiled.

"I'm listening," she said.

Victoria cleared her throat.

"Instead of turning over The Eternal Flame, I'll bring you The Fire Sword. I know that Vencrim has been looking for it."

Leveena stayed silent for a moment.

"You don't have it, do you?" Leveena asked.

Victoria shook her head.

"No..." she started, "But we will. We just need time to retrieve it."

Leveena thought for a few moments. She seemed interested.

"Okay," Leveena said with a smile. "I accept. You have three days to find the sword."

Leveena ran her finger across King Finnian's face, lightly cutting him.

"Don't be late," Leveena taunted.

The hologram ended. Victoria pushed a few buttons on the dashboard of the jet until a hologram appeared. It displayed a countdown that started at seventy-two hours.

"We need to hurry," Victoria said. "It'll be nearly impossible to find the sword in three days."

Matthew cleared his throat.

"Victoria," he started, "You asked me if I'd sacrifice everything for Valor. You asked me to become The Eternal Flame, and you told me that you'd fight by my side. Well, I will."

Victoria looked at Matthew.

"As long as Lord Vencrim is alive," Matthew said, "I won't stop fighting. I will protect Valor with everything I have. I won't stop until Vencrim is defeated."

Victoria began to smile.

“And I,” Victoria promised, “will be there with you every step of the way, and I will fight by your side until my dying breath.”

Matthew smiled. This would be a dangerous journey. He would most likely die, but he at least knew that Victoria was with him. For the first time in his life, Matthew didn’t feel alone anymore.

Chapter Four: Neon City

Matthew watched the bright colors of space pass by as he sat in Victoria's jet. It was just like the night before, only this time he wasn't under the influence of a tranquilizer. Victoria noticed Matthew watching the huge planets and billions of stars. He had that magic twinkle in his eyes that someone gets while seeing the beauty of space for the first time.

"It's beautiful, isn't it?" Victoria asked.

Matthew nodded.

"It's incredible," he replied as he turned to Victoria. "Is traveling across space always this amazing?"

Victoria smiled.

"Sometimes," she replied, "usually. But there are some parts of space that I don't like going to... dark places with no planets or stars that are completely devoid of sound and light. It's terrifying."

Matthew shuddered. He hoped that he would never have to go there.

"That sounds terrifying," Matthew admitted. "Where are we going right now?"

Victoria swerved to dodge a meteor.

“I have a weapons supplier on a planet called Zikanos. He’ll give us food, money, and weapons. But I should warn you: this planet is dangerous. It has no sun, so it’s always nighttime. People have built an artificial civilization based on a life of pleasure. There are no trees, only internet towers. No houses, only clubs and bars. Criminals and junkies come here to relax.”

Matthew swallowed. This sounded like a great place.

• • •

After several hours of flying, Zikanos became visible from the jet. Most of it was large and dark, but one area was bright, and it glowed with different colored lights.

“That’s Neon City,” Victoria explained. “That’s where we're going.”

As they neared the city, Matthew saw that it was lit up by millions of billboards, signs, and even lights from flying cars. Loud music played in the distance. It looked like a huge party was going on.

“We’re almost there,” Victoria announced, “get ready to move out.”

Matthew unbuckled his seat belt as Victoria landed the jet on top of a large building, which held tons of other spaceships and jets.

“Let’s go,” Victoria said.

As they walked out of the jet, Matthew slipped and fell to the ground. Embarrassed, Matthew quickly stood back up. Victoria looked at him and smiled. Blushing, Matthew chuckled. There was something about Victoria’s smile that Matthew liked.

Or maybe he just liked her. Matthew wasn't sure yet. He tried not to think about it. Now wasn't a good time for that. Victoria pressed a button on her gauntlet, causing the jet to activate its cloaking mode. Matthew gasped as the ship became completely invisible.

"Let's go find the supplier," Victoria said.

Matthew and Victoria walked down the damp streets of Neon City. Tall skyscrapers rose to hundreds of floors, and many of these skyscrapers had bright neon lights. Different kinds of music could be heard all around, as if different groups were having different parties. Matthew noticed that not everybody here was human. Some people were actually aliens, some tall with green skin and some short and furry. Matthew gasped as he took everything in. He was actually on a futuristic alien planet.

"This has to be a dream..." Matthew said to himself.

Distracted, Matthew bumped into a tall human with a cybernetic eye.

"Watch it!" he growled.

"Sorry," Matthew said quickly.

Victoria moved closer to Matthew.

"Don't draw too much attention to yourself," Victoria said. "Vencrim's robots could already be here looking for us."

Matthew stayed silent. He noticed a yellow robot standing nearby. It could have belonged to Vencrim, but Matthew wasn't sure.

"Okay," he whispered, mostly to himself.

Victoria walked up to a building with a long garage door. A tall man in dark clothes stopped Victoria from entering.

"Name?" he demanded.

"Victoria McCallaghan," she replied.

“Business?” the man asked.

“We’re here to see The Supplier,” Victoria answered.

The man then started speaking in the Valorian language. Victoria replied, also in the same language. The man then pressed a button which opened the door. Victoria and Matthew entered the room.

“What did he say to you?” Matthew asked.

“He told me part of a Valorian proverb,” she replied. "There is no direct translation to English, but it basically says, ‘the one who has fire... can either help or destroy’. It’s inspired by The Eternal Flame, but it mainly means that you should take the gifts you’ve been given in life and use them to help others instead of yourself.”

Matthew looked down at his hands. He had been given power. So far, he had used them for good. He just hoped that he could be powerful enough to save King Finnian when the time came.

“Victoria!” a man exclaimed happily.

Matthew and Victoria turned to see a tall man with a metal right hand. He also wore some kind of tactical vest. The man walked over to Victoria and hugged her.

“It has been so long,” the man said.

“I know,” Victoria replied, “but I’m here under terrible circumstances. My father has been kidnapped by Lord Leveena. She’s taken the castle.”

The man gasped as he sat down in a metal armchair.

“Those are bad circumstances,” he admitted.

“It’s not hopeless yet,” Victoria said. “We made Leveena a deal. We have two days to bring her the Fire Sword before she kills my father. She has the castle, but we found The Eternal Flame."

The man stood up.

"You've found The Eternal Flame?!" he asked her excitedly.

Victoria nodded.

"Is he here?" he asked anxiously.

"He's right here," she answered

"Where?"

Confused, Matthew turned to look at Victoria as The Supplier began to look around the room.

"I'm right here," Matthew said.

The Supplier gasped.

"YOU are The Eternal Flame?!" he asked Matthew, clearly shocked for some reason.

"I think so," Matthew answered.

The Supplier walked over to Matthew. He took out a silver rope and began measuring him.

"You are shorter than I imagined," The Supplier stated.

Matthew just stood there awkwardly.

"Okay..." he said.

Victoria chuckled.

"Matthew, this is The Supplier. Supplier, this is Matthew, The Eternal Flame."

The Supplier extended his metal hand toward Matthew.

"A pleasure to meet you, your highness," the Supplier said.

"You can just call me Matthew," he replied.

"Perfect," the Supplier said as he turned to Victoria. "How can I be of assistance today?"

Victoria answered, "We need some supplies. Food, clothes, and weapons, if you have them."

The Supplier giggled mischievously.

"Of course I have them," he replied. "I have a few crates in the back."

The Supplier walked over to the back of the room. He returned a few minutes later with two black backpacks and two large crates.

"Here we are," he said. "Food, clothes, and weapons. I also put a few extra goodies in the packs."

Victoria smiled.

"Thank you," she said as she hugged him. "We owe you bigtime."

The Supplier waved her off.

"You owe me nothing," he said. "It is a pleasure to serve the Princess of Valor and The Eternal Flame. May the stars burn brightly for you tonight. Oh, once you defeat Leveena, you'll have to come back and tell me all about it!"

Matthew and Victoria left the Supplier's warehouse. Each put on a backpack and pushed a crate. The crates hovered off the ground, so they were no trouble to push. Victoria cut through a dark alley to avoid the people on the main streets. She parked the crate nearby and told Matthew to stop.

"Before we continue," Victoria started, "I should at least teach you the basics of your powers and how to use them. If you face Leveena again soon, she will kill you."

Matthew took off his backpack and set it on top of his crate.

"How do I use my powers?" he asked.

Victoria sat down on the ground and closed her eyes. Matthew did the same.

"Think of something that calms you," Victoria said, "something that relaxes you when you're stressed."

Matthew took a deep breath. What made him calm? He tried to focus, but his mind started racing. He tried to imagine the white snow on Valor, but he saw glimpses of Leveena destroying the castle. He tried to focus on Waldo, but he saw the fire that almost killed him. He tried to concentrate on becoming a hero, but instead, he saw Lord Vencrim and his massive robot army. Matthew was awoken from his vision by Victoria, who had splashed a bucket of water on him. Matthew coughed and choked on the water. He saw that the water was sizzling on his skin.

"What happened?" Matthew asked.

"You were on fire," Victoria replied.

Matthew wiped the water from his eyes.

"Is that a good thing?" he asked.

"No," Victoria replied sternly, "not like that. You were on fire, but it wasn't contained. The flames were erratic and dangerous. If you can't control the fire, it will control you."

Matthew looked down at the ground. Victoria noticed Matthew's sadness and regretted speaking so angrily to him. After all, this was his first try.

"I'm sorry, Matthew," Victoria said. "But your powers are really dangerous. You could hurt yourself or somebody else. I just want to make sure that doesn't happen. Let's try again."

Matthew closed his eyes. Another set of chaotic and scary images passed through his mind, but he pushed them out. Instead, he thought about something good without allowing fear to creep in. This time, Matthew imagined the waves of the ocean and how they moved so forcefully, yet so peacefully.

"Extend your hand," Victoria commanded.

Matthew extended his hand, which felt warm.

“Open your eyes,” Victoria said.

Matthew opened his eyes to find a small fire burning on his palm. The fire was small and calm, not large and erratic like the other ones.

“Woah...” Matthew said in awe.

The fire was touching him, but it didn’t burn him. It just felt like a gentle warmth. Victoria stood up. She pointed to a row of cans and bottles that she had set up on a garbage bin.

“Try to hit the bottles,” Victoria said.

Matthew aimed at the bottles and threw the small fire. The fire, not very strong, quickly died out in the air.

“It’s okay,” Victoria said. “Try again. This time, try to add more fire to the fire, molding it into a ball.”

Matthew took a deep breath as he created another flame. Then he made one in his other hand. He mixed them together like dough and created a ball of fire. It was mostly round, but it was still changing and moving like a normal fire. Since the fireball was a combination of two small flames, it was hotter and brighter than a normal flame. Matthew threw the fireball at the bottles, knocking one down.

“I did it!” he exclaimed.

Victoria smiled at him.

“Great job,” she said, “but try it one more time. Make the fireball even stronger, but only use one hand. Then throw it as hard as you can without using physical force.”

Matthew looked down at his hand as he tried to understand Victoria’s instructions. He created the fire as usual, but how could he add to it without using his other hand? Matthew focused on the fire. He noticed that he could make it a little taller just by thinking about it. Using just his mind, Matthew bent the fire onto itself. Now Matthew was creating a fireball by increasing the size of the flame while placing the extra fire onto itself, creating a dense swirling fireball. He did this for a few seconds until the fireball was as bright as a lightbulb. Now he had a ball of concentrated fire. Matthew looked up at the bottles. How could he throw it without using physical strength? Matthew thought it through for a second. He already knew he could move the fire with his mind, so maybe he could increase the speed of the fireball while it was in the air. Matthew lightly threw the fireball at the bottles. Matthew focused on pushing the ball toward the bottle. He focused as hard as he could. As soon as the fireball left his hand, it rocketed toward the bottles at an incredible speed, breaking through a bottle and through the wall behind it. The bottle had shattered so hard that pieces of glass had projected everywhere nearby, even breaking through all of the other bottles. The fireball had drilled a small hole behind the bottles, showing the inside of the building.

"You did it!" Victoria exclaimed.

Matthew laughed and cheered. Excited, they hugged each other in celebration. They laughed for a moment before they realized that the hug was a little awkward, so they let go. Matthew cleared his throat, and Victoria partially turned away.

"Great job," Victoria said with a smile.

"Thanks," Matthew said.

He looked at Victoria. It looked like she had hope for her father now. With more training, maybe they would stand a chance against Leveena.

A huge booming sound cut through the silence. Matthew and Victoria looked up at the sky. A small object flew through the sky, followed by another boom and another object.

“What is that?” Matthew asked.

Victoria pushed a button on her gauntlet and magnified the object. She saw that the object was a small rocket that was speeding toward Neon City. The rocket had a familiar symbol on it. It was the letter V in a language called Nevenhi, Lord Vencrim’s native language. Victoria’s jaw dropped.

“It’s two of Lord Vencrim’s Destroyer robots,” she said quickly. “We need to get out of here now.”

Matthew grabbed his backpack and put it on. He and Victoria then grabbed the crates and began pushing them toward the jet.

• • •

The giant rocket landed in the streets of Neon City, breaking through part of the street. The people nearby began to crowd around it, unsure of what it was. The rocket then began to creak and hum as the outer plates of the rocket began to slide away, revealing a giant metal hand reaching out of the ship. The hand grabbed onto the street as a giant robot followed. The people nearby continued to watch. The robot stood up. It was at least fifteen feet tall. The robot looked around at the people, scanning them all.

TARGET: THE ETERNAL FLAME.
TARGET NOT FOUND.
TARGET: VICTORIA MCCALLAGHAN.
TARGET NOT FOUND.

SOLUTION: DRAW TARGETS OUT OF HIDING.

The robot activated a thick beam of lasers from its eyes, destroying nearby buildings. People began to panic and run away from the area. Another rocket landed nearby, causing even more panic. The two robots began to mercilessly destroy everything in their paths.

• • •

"Keep running!" Victoria shouted.

Matthew continued to push the crate toward the jet. He could see the building now. The invisible jet was hidden on top.

"We're almost there!" Matthew called.

Before they could reach the building, a Destroyer crashed down in front of them, shaking the ground. The Destroyer had rockets on its feet like Victoria's boots, which allowed it to fly and land in front of them. Victoria and Matthew fell to the ground because of the impact. The Destroyer scanned the two.

MATCH: VICTORIA MCCALLAGHAN.
MATCH: THE ETERNAL FLAME.
TARGETS FOUND.
OBJECTIVE: DESTROY TARGETS.

The robot's eyes began to glow red as it activated its lasers.

"Move!" Victoria shouted as she rolled away.

Matthew did the same. The laser beam shot out of the robot, hitting the spot where Matthew and Victoria were lying a moment before. The crates, which were still there, were destroyed by the beam. Matthew watched in fear as their supplies were destroyed right in front of them. Victoria activated her helmet.

"Run!" she shouted to Matthew.

Victoria rocketed toward the robot with her boots. She tried to punch it in the face, but the robot backhanded her, hitting her through the window of a nearby building. The robot scanned the building. It couldn't read any lifeforms. Victoria then ran out of the building holding a metal rod in her hand. Before the Destroyer could react, Victoria jumped up and pushed the rod through one of the Destroyer's eyes. The robot started malfunctioning and glitching. It mistakenly assumed that Victoria was still inside the building. The Destroyer lifted its hand and launched it like a missile. The hand crashed through the building, destroying everything in its path. Victoria had landed safely on the ground. The Destroyer's hand returned to it, reattaching itself to the arm. The robot noticed Victoria on the ground, so it used its remaining laser to hit the ground in front of her. Several large rocks were thrown at Victoria from the laser's damage. Victoria quickly moved to dodge them, but she was hit by a large rock, which knocked her over. The robot scanned Victoria and aimed its laser. Matthew jumped in between Victoria and the Destroyer. He created a fireball with his hand and threw it at the robot. The fireball shot through the air until it hit the Destroyer's last operational eye, destroying it. The laser was still running, so the beam activated. Since both of the Destroyer's eyes were damaged, the beam had nowhere to escape, causing the robot's head to explode from the pressure. Pieces of metal flew everywhere as the robot's body fell to the ground.

"Thank you," Victoria said, out of breath.

"Thank me later," Matthew said as he helped her to her feet.

Victoria used her gauntlet to control her jet, which flew over to them.

"How much supplies do we have left?" Victoria asked Matthew.

"Just the backpacks," Matthew answered.

"It'll have to do," Victoria said.

The jet landed in front of Matthew and Victoria as the cloaking system tuned off. The second Destroyer landed nearby. Matthew and Victoria ran into the jet.

"Here we go," Victoria said as they flew toward the sky.

The second Destroyer flew up into the air and began to follow them.

"That thing is right behind us!" Matthew said.

Victoria had already reached space, but the Destroyer continued to follow them. The robot lifted its arm toward them.

"I have an idea," Victoria said. "I can create a hologram of the ship, but I can't do that and pilot at the same time. I need you to take over."

Matthew put his hands on the co-pilot yoke.

"I don't know how to fly," he said.

"All I need you to do is push downward on the yoke," Victoria answered. "I'll create the hologram and cloak the ship."

The robot launched its metal hand at the jet.

"Now!" Victoria yelled.

The robot watched as the metal hand hit the ship, blowing it up. The robot stopped and floated in space, scanning the debris.

NO LIFEFORMS DETECTED.
OBJECTIVE: COMPLETE.

The Destroyer reattached its hand and flew away.

"Did it work?" Matthew asked.

Victoria nodded.

"It worked," she said.

She pressed a few buttons on the dashboard. The pieces of debris in the sky above them disappeared. The jet came out of cloaking as it reappeared several yards away from the fake debris.

"The Destroyer thought it hit us," Victoria explained, "but since we simultaneously created a hologram, cloaked the ship, and dived downwards, we moved out of the way while making it seem like we had been hit."

Matthew sighed.

"That's incredible," he said.

Victoria opened her backpack. She pulled out a black sword hilt that was decorated with a purple ring. Victoria pressed a button on the handle, which caused a long silver blade to extend outwards from the top.

"A collapsible sword... this is perfect," she said. "I wasn't able to grab any weapons earlier."

Victoria pressed the button again, hiding the blade. She attached the hilt to the black belt on her armor. Matthew pulled out a round device from his backpack.

"What does this do?" he asked.

"That's a Disabler," she answered. "Once you push the button, you throw it at a robot. The magnet on the bottom will cause it to stick to the robot. After that, the device will electrocute the robot, which will short circuit and die."

Matthew studied the small device.

"This will be perfect then," he answered.

Aside from the weapons, Matthew and Victoria also found a small ration of food and ten different kinds of currencies.

"We'll have to make do with this," Victoria said.

Matthew nodded.

"Where are we going next?" he asked.

Victoria started up the jet.

"Our next destination is a planet called Exorda. There we should be able to learn the location of the Fire Sword."

Victoria pressed a button on the dashboard, bringing up the countdown. Sixty-three hours remained.

"Let's hurry," Victoria said quietly.

The jet shot forward at full speed toward Exorda. Matthew hoped that they would make it in time.

Chapter 5: The Wizard

Matthew stared out of the side window of Victoria's jet.

"I don't mean to bother you," Matthew started, "but are we almost there yet?"

Matthew hadn't considered that space travel could take so long.

"Not yet," Victoria answered patiently. "It's going to be a few more hours. I'm going as fast as I can."

Matthew watched as the jet passed by a large planet, which disappeared within seconds.

"Exactly how fast are we going?" he asked Victoria.

Victoria could tell that Matthew was impressed with the speed of the jet.

"Right now..." she started, "Two hundred million miles per hour."

Matthew stared at her in awe.

"Two hundred million?!" he asked.

Victoria smiled and nodded.

"What's the fastest ever flown?" Matthew asked.

Victoria pressed a few buttons on the dashboard of the jet. A hologram displayed several numbers and names.

"The speed of light is the fastest ever flown," Victoria explained. "It's about six hundred and seventy million miles per hour, but only Lord Vencrim has ever traveled that fast. I don't know how, but Vencrim found a way to majorly manipulate space-time. It's how he created the wormhole above Valor. At that speed, it might even be possible to travel through time."

Matthew didn't fully understand what Victoria told him, but he was interested and amazed. Victoria spent the next several hours telling Matthew all about space travel. She told him all about the special shields that her jet needed because of the dust in space. At high speeds, a single grain of dust could shoot through the ship like a bullet. The hours went by quickly until Matthew and Victoria finally arrived at their destination: the planet Exorda. Exorda was a small green planet with a few blue spots.

"Here we are," Victoria said as she landed the jet in the middle of a thick jungle.

Tall mossy trees covered most of the planet's surface. Matthew and Victoria walked out of the jet and stepped onto the muddy ground. This planet was warm and damp. Animal noises and bird callings could be heard in the distance.

"Let's go," Victoria said.

Matthew followed Victoria through the jungle.

"The Fire Temple shouldn't be too far," Victoria informed as she read her gauntlet's hologram map. "I made sure we were farther away just in case Leveena has robots waiting for us."

Matthew accidentally stepped into a deep mud puddle, covering his left boot in mud. He did not like this planet. As they walked along, Matthew thought of a question. He didn't really want to ask Victoria about it, but he thought now was as good a time as any.

"I wanted to ask you something..." Matthew started, "About Leveena."

Victoria looked at Matthew.

"What about her?" she asked.

"What exactly is she?" Matthew asked. "Is she a robot or some kind of human?"

Victoria didn't say anything at first, but she kept moving through the jungle.

"She used to be human," Victoria finally said. "Leveena once fought for my father. She was one of Valor's greatest warriors. Then Lord Vencrim found her and manipulated her. He gave her a taste of power, and she wanted more. Leveena devoted herself to Vencrim, and she even killed her own family, but…"

Victoria was silent for a moment.

"She didn't want to kill her family. She didn't even fully realize what she had done until they were already dead. She regretted what she'd done. Vencrim hated Leveena's 'weakness,' as he called it, so he killed her. He destroyed her human body and remade her into his most advanced robot. She suffered terribly..."

Matthew was quiet for a moment.

"Does she still think like a human?" he asked.

"Yes," Victoria replied. "She has all her old memories, so she's basically a human in a robot body. Her metal body gives her many advantages, but now she barely remembers what it feels like to be human. She's hated Vencrim ever since."

Matthew kept walking.

"Then why does she still serve him?" he asked.

Victoria stepped over a log.

"I think a part of her enjoys being evil. Part of her really likes to hurt and kill people because it makes her feel powerful. The other part is afraid. She knows that if she rebels against Lord Vencrim, he'll kill her."

Matthew could tell that Victoria didn't really want to talk about Leveena anymore. It was clearly a tough subject for her for some reason. Maybe Leveena and Victoria used to be friends? Matthew decided to just forget about it for now.

"We're almost there," Victoria said.

Matthew could see the top of a stone temple in the distance, which was shaped like a giant pyramid. The grey pyramid had several levels of stone, dozens of stairs, and a little room at the top.

"Look at this," Victoria said as she pointed to the ground.

Matthew looked down at the ground and saw a carving of a man with a flaming sword and shield fighting a giant red dragon. Matthew hoped that he wouldn't be fighting a dragon anytime soon. He walked over to the temple and began to walk up the stairs, but he noticed that Victoria didn't follow him.

"What is it?" Matthew asked.

"I can't come inside," Victoria said. "Only a Warrior of Fire can enter the temple."

Matthew looked up to the top.

"Okay," he said, "then let's hope I truly am The Eternal Flame."

Matthew continued to climb up the stairs. Once he reached the top, he noticed a skeleton lying on the ground near the door. The skeleton had partially burned away. This man wasn't a

Warrior of Fire. Matthew looked into the dark room. He slowly walked in, but nothing happened. He took one more step, but the ground cracked beneath him. The floor broke away as he fell down into the center of the temple. He cried out as he fell to the ground, hurting his foot. The room he was in now was dark at first, but several torches on the wall randomly flared up, illuminating a long hallway.

• • •

Outside, Victoria saw Matthew fall through the temple floor. She gasped as he dropped down to the ground. Victoria hoped that Matthew would be safe, but she was worried for him. Not just here and now, but also for the future. What if Lord Vencrim killed him? He probably would. Vencrim had killed several other Warriors of Fire before Matthew. Vencrim never showed mercy. Matthew would need to be ten times better than the other warriors to even stand a chance. Victoria sighed sadly. Matthew was different than the other warriors. He was gentle and kind. He truly wanted to protect Valor. Victoria hoped that these differences would truly make Matthew worthy of becoming The Eternal Flame.

• • •

Inside the temple, Matthew slowly limped through the long hallway. Drawn on the walls were hundreds of little cave pictures. They told some kind of story, but Matthew couldn't understand it. He continued walking until he reached the end of the hallway. The only thing there was a blank stone wall. Frustrated, Matthew turned around and started walking in the opposite direction. He walked until he reached the other end of the hallway, which was also a dead end. Matthew slunk to the ground. His foot hurt and he was tired. He couldn't find the way out. Even if he did, he didn't have the Fire Sword. Leveena would kill him for sure.

"It's hopeless," Matthew said to himself.

"It is only hopeless if you choose it to be," a voice said.

Matthew stood back up and looked down the dark hallway, but he couldn't see anybody.

"Who's there?" Matthew asked.

"A friend," the voice replied.

Matthew was worried, but the voice didn't sound threatening. It sounded old and calm. Maybe the voice was some kind of guardian of the temple.

"Please, sir," Matthew asked, "how do I find The Fire sword?"

"Look to the past, and you can learn your future," the voice said.

"What does that mean?" Matthew asked.

The voice said nothing. Matthew sighed and turned toward the wall. He had an idea. His visions might've shown him the future, so maybe he could control it. Matthew placed his hand on the wall and tried to focus. He closed his eyes, but he could only see darkness. Matthew opened his eyes. He looked at the wall and found that the pictures began to move. The entire wall came to life as the images began to tell their story. Several little men fought against one larger man, but the large man destroyed them all. The man then fought against a burning man, but he defeated him as well. Then he fought another burning man, and another, and another. He killed them all. Finally came a boy who was burned in a fire protecting a baby. He burst into flames and fought several of the large man's metal soldiers. The boy then entered a giant red castle that hid a sword in a pile of gold. A giant dragon appeared and breathed fire at him. The boy tried to grab the sword. The dragon's fire reached the boy just as he reached the sword. The pictures on the wall stopped moving. Matthew couldn't tell if the boy had reached the sword in time or if he had been burned alive.

"That's me, isn't it?" Matthew asked.

"It could be," the voice replied. "You could continue looking into your future, but you might not like what you find."

Matthew placed his hand on the picture of himself.

"I want to know..." Matthew started, "but it might change my mind about protecting Valor. I might decide to run and hide instead of fighting Vencrim."

Matthew turned away from the wall.

"I don't want to know," he finally said, "but... just tell me this... will Victoria be okay?"

The voice waited a moment before answering.

"She will be safe as long as you protect her," the voice assured.

Matthew looked back at the wall. A small purple figure fought bravely against two giant robots near the dragon's castle.

"Then I'll always protect her," Matthew promised.

Looking to the side, Matthew noticed that the picture of The Fire Sword was outlined in the stone. Matthew pressed his hand on the picture, which sank into the wall. The walls began to split open as a doorway to another room was formed. Inside the room sat an old man. The man had a long white beard. He wore a long hat and a long dark robe, which had stars in space that twinkled in the darkness.

"Welcome, Matthew," the man greeted warmly.

His voice was the same as the voice in the hallway.

"My name is Majesto," he said. "It is good to meet you."

Matthew shook the man's outstretched hand.

"I think I've heard about you," Matthew said. "You fought Lord Vencrim, didn't you?"

Majesto nodded.

"I did," he answered, "but I couldn't defeat him. Instead, I looked into the future, and I found you: The Eternal Flame. I knew that if anybody could defeat him, it would be you... well, you and your friends."

Matthew was confused.

"Which friends?" he asked.

Majesto smiled.

"You'll meet them soon enough," he said. "Well, I don't have the Fire Sword here. It has been hidden so that Vencrim cannot find it. Take this."

Majesto pulled a map out of the sleeve of his robe and handed it to Matthew.

"This map will show you how to get to Rovunt. There is another temple there, one that holds the key to the true Fire Temple on Lahtaris."

Matthew sighed. He would need to travel to two more planets before he could find the sword. Time was running out for King Finnian. Matthew rolled up the map and put it in his backpack.

“Thank you,” Matthew said to Majesto.

“You’re welcome,” he said. “One more thing...”

Majesto pulled his wand from his robe.

“Lord Vencrim doesn't know that I am alive, and I would like to keep it that way. Please, tell no one that I was here.”

“I won’t tell a soul,” Matthew promised.

Majesto smiled.

“I had a feeling you’d say that,” he joked.

Majesto waved his wand, sending bright sparks up into the air. Majesto’s wand had a large white crystal in it, which began to glow. Mathew was momentarily blinded by the bright light that filled the room.

“I will see you again soon,” Majesto said as the room turned black.

Matthew woke up at the bottom of the temple. He looked up to find the broken floor he had fallen through. He could feel the map in his pocket, so he knew that he hadn’t been dreaming. Matthew noticed an old ladder on the wall, so he used it to escape. Victoria met him at the bottom of the temple stairs.

“Are you okay?” she asked.

“Yeah,” Matthew answered. “I’m fine.”

Victoria noticed that Matthew was empty-handed.

“Did you find The Fire Sword?” she asked him.

Matthew shook his head and handed her the map.

“This was all I could get,” he said.

Victoria read the map with a worried expression.

“We need to hurry,” she said. “Rovunt is very far away.”

•••

On the way back to the jet, Matthew decided to continue his earlier conversations with Victoria. Matthew didn't know why, but he was worried for her. Her father had been kidnapped and her house was taken over. In the end, it was up to her to set things right. This must have been the worst day of her life. Matthew decided to ask Victoria random questions in hopes of cheering her up.

"Victoria..." Matthew started.

"Yeah?" she answered.

"What's your favorite color?" he asked.

Victoria glanced at him and chuckled. She had been expecting a more serious question.

"Purple," she said with a smirk, "the color of royalty."

Matthew smiled.

"What's yours?" she asked him.

"Red," he replied, "the color of fire."

Victoria chuckled.

"Fire is orange," she corrected.

Matthew lifted his hand. He created a small flame, which burned yellow and orange.

"Oh..." he said, embarrassed.

Victoria laughed quietly.

"Told you so," she said.

Matthew laughed.

"Okay," he continued, "what's your favorite weapon?"

"Hm..." Victoria started. "Probably a sword."

Matthew nodded.

"I haven't tried very many weapons, but I think I'll like The Fire Sword."

A two-tailed monkey jumped from one tree to the other above Victoria.

"What is your favorite animal?" she asked Matthew.

"Probably a wolf… maybe a dragon," Matthew answered. "What about you?"

Victoria smiled.

"I like horses," she said.

"Horses?" Matthew repeated.

"Yeah," she said. "I know it probably sounds typical for a teenage princess to like horses, but they're so majestic. I've ridden into great battles on horses."

Matthew tried to imagine Victoria in her purple armor fighting with her retractable sword on a horse on a large battlefield.

"That does sound pretty majestic," Matthew admitted.

Victoria noticed the jet in the distance.

"Here we are," she said.

Matthew saw a few words written on the side of the jet in Valorian. He hadn't noticed it before, mainly since he hadn't really had the time to look over the jet. The metal boarding platform lowered itself to the ground.

"What does this say?" he asked Victoria as they walked in.

"It's the name of the jet," Victoria answered. "On Valor, it's customary for a captain to name their ship."

Matthew strapped himself into his seat.

"What did you name your jet?" he asked her.

Victoria smiled as she flew up toward space.

"The Majesty," she answered.

Matthew smiled.

"It's perfect," he said.

Victoria began to blush.

"Thank you," she said.

Matthew unrolled the map that Majesto had given him.

"Next stop," Matthew said, "Rov..."

Matthew was interrupted as the jet violently jerked to the side.

"What was that?" he asked.

Victoria pushed a button on the dashboard. Part of the front windshield worked as a screen to display what was happening behind The Majesty. A Destroyer was hot on their tail, and it had already used its rocket hand to hit the back of the ship. The white eyes of the Destroyer began to glow red.

"Oh, no..." Victoria said.

The Destroyer used its laser to hit the back of the Majesty. The ship began to lose power as the thrusters began to break apart. Matthew could feel the cold of space seeping into the jet.

"The ship's going to explode," Victoria explained quickly. "I need to set her down."

A small blue planet was visible nearby.

"There's a planet right there," Matthew said.

Victoria flew toward the planet. The Destroyer followed them.

"I have an idea," she said. "Hold on tight."

Victoria looked worried. Matthew knew she was a great pilot, but that would be tested right now. Victoria dove straight down toward the planet. Water covered most of the planet, but Victoria was aiming directly for a small strip of land.

"Victoria..." Matthew said nervously.

"Wait..." she said.

The Destroyer was getting closer, and so was the ground.

"Victoria!" Matthew exclaimed.

The ground was right in front of them.

"Now!" Victoria shouted as she pulled on the yoke.

The jet barely missed the ground as Victoria pulled with all her strength. Only a small part of the back thrusters scraped the ground. The Destroyer that was right behind them crashed straight into the ground at full speed, immediately crushing and destroying it.

"That was amazing!" Matthew exclaimed excitedly.

Victoria smiled. The excitement ended as the back thrusters exploded, throwing the jet to the ground. Victoria tried to use the jet as a glider as she pulled up. Matthew and Victoria groaned as the Majesty crashed through several trees and rocks. The ship hit a large boulder, which flipped the entire jet. The Majesty tumbled and rolled onto the ground several times before it finally stopped on a beach. The jet was almost completely destroyed. Inside the Majesty, Victoria sat unconscious in her seat, blood on her forehead. Matthew turned toward her. He struggled to open his eyes. He felt drowsy since he had also hit his head in the crash. The last thing he saw was Victoria, injured and asleep.

"Victoria..." he started.

But he was unconscious before he could finish.

Chapter Six:
Dowah

Matthew slowly woke up. His eyes felt heavy, and his head was throbbing.

"Victoria..." he whispered.

There was no answer. Matthew felt dizzy. He noticed that he was gently swaying back and forth. He saw that he was hanging upside down from the ceiling of a small cave. Matthew studied his surroundings. The back of the cave was dark, but light came in from the front. The ground was covered in sand, and tall rocks came up from it. Matthew's green jacket and black boots sat on a small stone shelf. A row of a dozen large tiki masks stood in front of the cave. Matthew gasped as the tiki masks blinked. There were people behind them, dark-skinned natives who raised their spears at Matthew. He tried to break out of the trap he was hanging from, but he couldn't move his arms.

"Where is Victoria?" Matthew asked.

The man with the largest mask stepped forward. The mask was tall and brown; it covered half of the man's entire body. The mask made clicking sounds as it randomly rotated to the side. It would click again as it returned to its normal position.

"I am Kun-Alu, the Tiki King. Who are you?" the man spoke.

Matthew tried to free his arms.

“I am Matthew, The Eternal Flame,” Matthew replied.

The tiki men looked at each other and began to laugh.

“You are The Eternal Flame?” the king asked in disbelief.

“Where is Victoria?” Matthew asked angrily.

Kun-Alu said something in another language to his men, who laughed. Matthew heated up his hands. The ropes that held him caught fire and broke, dropping Matthew to the sandy ground. Matthew landed on his right foot and his left knee. He held large flames in his hands, and his eyes began to glow red. The flames cast an orange color on the walls of the cave.

“Where is she?!” Matthew growled. “I won’t ask again.”

The tiki men were instantly afraid, so they placed their spears in the sand and kneeled before Matthew. Matthew stopped the flames and stood up. The Tiki King stepped forward again.

“I apologize,” he said to Matthew “we didn’t know... I thought you were blaspheming The Eternal Flame. Your friend is over here. Come, follow me.”

The king brought Matthew outside of the small cave. Matthew saw miles of ocean all around him, with sand at his feet. He was on a tropical island.

“Where am I?” Matthew asked calmly.

By now he realized that these people meant no harm to him or Victoria.

Kun-Alu's mask rotated to the side.

“You are on Dowah, the ocean planet,” he answered. “This is Ottaka, the Mother Island.”

Matthew knew that Dowah wasn’t on the list of planets he needed to visit soon. Crashing here would waste tons of valuable time. Matthew followed the king to another small cave, where

Victoria slept on a bed of palm leaves. Her wrists were tied to the bed, and she had a bandage wrapped around her head. Her armor had a few small areas where the purple paint had been scratched off.

"She was injured in the crash," the king said, "but she is okay."

Matthew nodded. He walked over to Victoria and held her limp armored hand.

"What happened to the jet?" Matthew asked.

Kun-Alu took Matthew to the jet, which was terribly damaged. The entire rear thruster was destroyed, and most of the right side was missing. The Majesty wasn't going to be flying anytime soon.

"What are we going to do?" Matthew asked himself.

They were running out of time.

"We can fix it," the king started, "but we must ask something of you first."

Matthew looked at the king.

"What do you need?" Matthew asked.

The king's wooden mask rotated sideways.

"We had possession of a magical gem called the Eye of Calypso, but it was stolen from us by Arach-Anach, our great enemy. Arach-Anach took the gem to his cave in the dark mountain pass. The gem creates a shield around our land whenever a tsunami approaches. Without it, we are vulnerable and at risk of being destroyed. A tsunami has already been spotted many miles away. We only have an hour left before it hits. If you could find the gem, we would forever be in your debt."

Matthew looked toward the nearby mountains. A large dark crack cut through the middle. That was the mountain pass. The gem was in there. Matthew thought for a second. With Victoria unconscious, he would have to make his own decision. Matthew walked over to the jet and turned on the countdown. A glitching hologram displayed fifty-three, then fifty-two. Matthew thought about King Finnian. He was counting on Victoria and Matthew. Matthew couldn't let him down.

"Okay," Matthew said to the king. "I'll find the gem, but you need to get started on the ship immediately."

The king's mask rotated until it was upside down.

"Thank you," he said. "We will start immediately."

The king shouted at some men in grass skirts who came over and started fixing the ship.

Matthew walked back to Victoria. She was still asleep.

"I'm going to go find the king's gem," Matthew said to Victoria, who he knew couldn't hear him.

Matthew moved away a strand of Victoria's hair that was on her face.

"Wake up soon, okay?" he said worriedly.

Matthew walked out of the cave and onto the beach. The bright blue waters sat calmly in the sea. Dozens of small islands were visible in the area. Palm trees were scattered all along the coast. It reminded Matthew of the beach in San Diego.

"Are you ready for your journey?" the Tiki King asked Matthew.

"I'm ready," Matthew answered as he finished putting on his boots. "Do you have any weapons I could take with me?"

Kun-Alu called out to a few men who brought Matthew a metal spear.

“Take this,” the king said. “May it serve you well.”

Matthew thanked the king and began to walk through the jungle toward the mountains. Different kinds of large trees were scattered all over. The trees were thick enough to cast a large shade over the jungle floor, making the temperature cooler than the beach. It was still too warm for Matthew to wear his jacket, so he left it behind. Now he wore his black pants and boots, along with his plain black t-shirt. In the forest, little streams of water flowed in different directions, and giant logs sat in various places. Matthew came across a large tiki mask that had a large crack in it. The mask had a giant green eye printed on the forehead. The eye was looking to the left, so Matthew decided to walk in that direction. He soon found another mask, then another. He eventually came to a large river. A mask stood right by the edge. The eye was looking over the river. Matthew looked at the water. It was flowing fast, too fast to swim across. The other side of the river was at least twenty feet away. It was way too far to jump across. Unless... Matthew threw the spear over to the other side. He then started walking backward. He needed to gain enough speed. Matthew took a deep breath. He ran toward the river as fast as he could. He yelled as he jumped high, facing his hands toward the ground. He shot fire from his hands, focusing as much power as he could. The fire acted like small thrusters that kept Matthew from falling too quickly. Matthew was only in the air for a few seconds, but it felt like a minute. He was almost there... Matthew stuck his foot out toward the ground. He made it. Matthew laughed as he landed safely on the ground. He pulled the spear out of the ground and continued walking toward the mountain pass.

• • •

Matthew soon found a small village. He saw dozens of small houses that were made of wood with straw roofs. This village was empty; it had been completely abandoned.

"Hello?" Matthew called.

Nobody answered. Matthew noticed large spiderwebs on a few of the houses. One web stretched from the roof of a house all the way to the ground.

"Must've been one big spider," Matthew said to himself.

Matthew noticed a large statue in the center of the village. It was of a woman standing in the sea. One of her eyes was missing from the statue.

"Calypso..." Matthew said to himself. "This must be where the gem goes."

Matthew looked at the mountains. He was almost there. Matthew hoped that Arach-Anach, whoever he was, wasn't home. Matthew continued toward the mountains.

After another few minutes of walking, Matthew reached the mountain pass. The crack looked much larger up close, reaching about half a mile up the mountain. The mouth of the cave was covered in more webs.

"Arach... oh, no..." Matthew said to himself as he took a few steps back. "It's a giant spider!"

Matthew cracked his knuckles and stretched his back. He wasn't afraid of spiders, but he might be after this. Matthew heard a quiet cracking noise behind him. He turned toward the sea and saw a large wave in the distance. The wave crashed through a small island, leaving it completely empty as it passed over it. Not a single tree was left standing on the island. The tsunami continued through the water. It was on a direct collision course with the Mother Island.

"I need to hurry," Matthew said to himself as he walked into the cave.

Matthew tried using the spear to cut through the spiderwebs, but it was difficult since the webs kept sticking to the spear. Instead, Matthew decided to melt the webs with his fire. He realized that this was way faster than cutting them with the spear. Through a crack in the webs, Matthew saw a glowing light. He burned through the last few webs until he found a huge cave filled with tons of shiny and glowing objects. He saw a golden sword and a giant white diamond. Two tall pillars stood at the end of the dark room. In the center of the room sat a pedestal with a green gem that glowed brightly in the darkness. Matthew walked over to it. The gem reflected Matthew's eye back to him.

"This must be it," Matthew said as he reached for the gem.

Matthew heard a hissing noise in the shadows in front of him. He pulled his hand away from the gem and tightened his grip on the spear. A giant furry tarantula slowly crawled out of the shadows. The spider was about a foot taller than Matthew, and it had orange stripes on its legs. Matthew slowly stepped to the side. Matthew took a glance at the gem. He slowly reached his hand out toward it. The spider immediately ran toward Matthew, who quickly lifted his spear. The spider pounced on Matthew, but it fell on top of the spear, stabbing it completely through the head. The spider didn't even have time to shriek in pain. Matthew crawled out from under the heavy spider. He was covered in green goo.

"Disgusting!" Matthew said as he tried to wipe the goo off his shirt.

Matthew gave up and took his shirt off.

"That wasn't so bad," he said to himself, still shivering.

Matthew walked back over to the eye. He saw his own eye in the center, but he saw eight black eyes around the edges of the gem. A low growling voice in the cave made Matthew realize that this wasn't over yet. He looked up as the giant pillars at the end of the cave began to move. Matthew realized that they weren't pillars... they were spider legs! An enormous tarantula stepped out of the shadows. This spider was at least twenty feet tall. This was Arach-Anach. The spider hissed as it extended a leg toward Matthew, who jumped out of the way just before it crashed down on the ground. Matthew threw a fireball at the spider. The fireball hit the tarantula's head, but it did nothing. It only singed a bit of its thick fur. Matthew took a step backward.

"Uh-oh," he said to himself.

The spider swung another leg at Matthew, who was hit by it. Matthew was thrown against the cave wall. He fell to the ground on a pile of gold coins. Matthew noticed the golden sword, so he reached out for it. Arach-Anach shot a blanket of webs at Matthew, sticking his hand to the ground.

"No!" Matthew shouted.

He tried to burn out of the webs, but the tarantula continued to place more. Matthew was now completely stuck to the ground, unable to move. The spider walked over, its huge fangs dripping with venom. The spider quickly moved its mouth toward Matthew, who closed his eyes. The mouth of the cave suddenly glowed yellow as Victoria flew inside with her rocket boots. She yelled out as she lifted a spear toward the tarantula's mouth, cutting off its fangs. Arach-Anach screeched as it took a few steps backward.

"Are you okay?" Victoria asked Matthew as she helped cut him out of the webs.

"I'm okay," he said. "Are you okay?"

He moved Victoria's hair out of her face to reveal the bandage on her head. Victoria grabbed Matthew's wrist and nodded.

"I'm fine," she said. "How can I help?"

Matthew picked up the golden sword.

"There is a tsunami coming soon," Matthew said. "I need you to place the gem in the eye of the statue in the nearest village. The gem will create a shield around the island. I'll deal with the spider."

Victoria looked at the gem.

"On it," she said as her helmet covered her head.

Victoria ran toward the gem. The spider tried to hit her with its leg, but Victoria was too fast for it. Once she grabbed the gem, she used her boots to rocket out of the cave at full speed. The tarantula tried to follow her, but Matthew jumped in front of the mouth of the cave.

"I don't think so," Matthew said to Arach-Anach. "It's just you and me now."

Victoria flew through the forest toward the abandoned village. She could see the tsunami approaching quickly. It looked much larger up close. It was taller than the mountains on the island, and it was almost at the beach. Victoria found the statue. She flew up to the head of Calypso and placed the gem in the eye socket. The statue began to rumble as the gem unleashed a ball of energy. Victoria fell to the ground as the ball of energy began to expand through the island. The green energy stopped at the beach, just as the tsunami hit. The energy created a giant dome over the island. The giant wave of water hit the shield, but it didn't stop. The water kept pressing against the green energy. Victoria noticed that the shield began to crack. She looked at the gem, which also began to crack.

"Oh, no..." she said to herself.

Matthew held the golden sword and heated it with his hand. The handle and blade of the sword began to glow red with heat. The spider lunged toward Matthew, but he moved out of the way. He then used the sword to hit the spider's leg, cutting it off. The spider cried out in pain. It tried to strike Matthew again, but it only lost another leg. Matthew ran around the cave, swinging the sword at the spider. Leg by leg, Matthew dismembered the spider until it fell to the ground. Matthew slowly walked over to the tarantula.

"I'm sorry," he said to Arach-Anach as he lifted his sword, "but you're too much of a danger to these people."

Matthew pushed the hot glowing sword down into the spider's head, killing it. Victoria entered the cave.

"Matthew!" she called. "Come look at this!"

Matthew left the spiders in the cave, sword and spear still stabbed through the enemies of the Dowahns.

•••

Matthew looked up at the statue. The gem continued to crack. Matthew watched as water began to pour through the shield onto the beach.

"What do we do?" he asked Victoria.

"I don't know," she said.

Matthew climbed up onto the statue.

"I have an idea," he said.

Matthew placed his hand on the eye.

"I'm going to try to hold it together," he said.

Matthew focused his power to his hand. He held the gem, but it began to shake.

"It's not working," he said.

The gem shattered in his hand.

"No!" he yelled.

Water began to pour onto the beach. Matthew yelled out as he focused his full power into his fist. A new wave of energy came out from the statue, but it was red instead of green. The wave of energy stretched across the island until it reached the shore. The energy turned into a thick wall of fire that blocked off the water. Matthew didn't see it at the time, but Victoria saw that his eyes were glowing red. Matthew was tapping into his full potential.

"It's working!" Victoria told him.

The tsunami finally reached its end. The waves of water stopped pushing against the shields, so Matthew removed his hand from the eye socket of the statue.

"I can't believe that worked," Matthew said to Victoria.

Victoria smiled at him.

"You did it!" she said excitedly. "That was amazing!"

Matthew began to blush. Victoria looked down at her gauntlet.

"Now, let's get back to the Majesty," Victoria said.

• • •

On the beach, the tiki people ran toward Matthew and lifted him up on their shoulders. They began to chant and celebrate in another language. Some of the women threw flower necklaces around his neck. Matthew looked at Victoria, who was receiving the same treatment. The tiki king walked over to Matthew and Victoria.

"Eternal Flame, Princess of Valor," the king said, "we are eternally grateful to you. We have already started repairs on your jet, but it was badly damaged. Since it is not yet finished, I invite and encourage you to stay and spend the night with us. You can rest and celebrate with us before you return to your journey."

Matthew looked at Victoria. Victoria smiled and nodded.

"Just until the jet is finished," she answered.

The people cheered.

• • •

The people of Dowah sure knew how to throw a party. The sun set as everyone partied away. The Dowahns, having nearly died, celebrated the arrival of The Eternal Flame and the defeat of Arach-Anach. The king brought traditional clothes for Victoria and Matthew. Victoria was dressed in a grass skirt and a white cloth strapped around her chest. Matthew was still shirtless, but he now wore a grass skirt and brown boots. Kun-Alu also ordered a huge feast, which was quickly prepared. There was roasted porkilets with pink apples, three-eyed fried fish with pineapple, several different kinds of fruit, and a drink made with pineapple and coconut. Some of the food was human-like, but most of it was alien to Matthew. The porkilets was the best meat Matthew had ever tasted, but Victoria preferred the fish. Matthew had never tried yellow kiwis, which he loved.

"This is my new favorite fruit," Matthew said to the people, who began to cheer.

Matthew laughed. Of all the planets he had been to so far, this was his new favorite.

"Try this," Kun-Alu said as he handed a strip of meat to Matthew.

Matthew took a bite. The meat was tender and juicy.

"This is delicious," Matthew said. "What is it?"

"Arach-Anach," the king answered.

Matthew coughed and spat the meat out into a napkin.

"No, thank you," Matthew said, disgusted.

Victoria, who sat next to Matthew, laughed. Matthew smiled at her. Later in the night, the Tiki King started a game of limbo, which was a traditional game for the Dowahns. Everyone was encouraged to play. Matthew even convinced Victoria to join the game. Matthew had a slight advantage over everyone else since the limbo rod, which had been set on fire, couldn't hurt him. He did well in the first few rounds of the game, but Victoria ended up beating him. In the final round, only Kun-Alu and Victoria were left. The bar was set very low, only about two feet above the ground. Victoria laughed as she tried not to fall, but she fell anyway.

"Great try," Matthew said to her.

Victoria smiled. She was having a good time. The Tiki King walked over to the bar and began to twist and crack his arms. His mask twisted around several times before he bent his waist backward, walking perfectly under the bar. The people began to cheer for the king, who had beaten everyone else with his unnatural flexibility.

"Come," the king said to Matthew. "Let us play a game that you will surely win."

The king showed Matthew a new game, where you try to blow fire as far as you can. You take a drink of a flammable liquid and blow it at a flame, creating a bigger flame. Several Dowahns went first, but the tiki king created a huge flame that beat them all.

"Your turn," the king said to Matthew.

Matthew stepped up to the man who held the burning baton and the flammable drink. Matthew took the drink, but not the baton. Everyone began to murmur.

Victoria smiled in anticipation. Matthew took a mouthful of the drink and blew as hard as he could. At first, he only spit out the drink, but then it caught fire. The flame didn't extend outwards very far, but Matthew felt that he could make it bigger. He tried to growl and yell at the same time, and he accidentally coughed and breathed fire directly from his throat. Matthew breathed out the flames as it caused him to supernaturally roar like a monster. The flame extended outwards at least ten feet through the air before Matthew stopped it. Embarrassed, Matthew looked around at the people. The villagers were completely silent before they started cheering.

"You breathe fire like a dragon!" the king exclaimed as he raised Matthew's arm into the air. "That was spectacular!"

Matthew smiled. Victoria chuckled as she saw how proud Matthew was.

• • •

The night had mostly calmed down. People were scattered all around the beach. Most were asleep, but some quietly played volleyball or ate and drank at the bar. Another group of men took turns repairing The Majesty throughout the night. Victoria was sitting down on the beach making a crown of flowers, while Matthew sat at the bar with Kun-Alu. Matthew stared at Victoria as he sat.

"Do you like her?" the Tiki King asked as his mask rotated to the side.

"Like who?" Matthew asked. "Victoria?"

The king's mask rotated back to its original position.

"I have seen the way you look at her. Earlier today you were enraged when we didn't tell you where she was. You might've thought we had killed her, and you were very worried for her. You like her, don't you?"

Matthew looked back at Victoria.

"I don't know yet," he answered.

The King's mask rotated to the side again.

"You should go and talk to her," he said. "Here. Take her a drink. Tell her what you think of her."

He handed Matthew a cup of coconut pineapple punch as he pushed him out of his seat.

"I don't really..." Matthew protested.

"Just go," the king said.

Matthew started walking toward Victoria, but he looked back at the king. Kun-Alu motioned his hands excitedly toward Victoria. Matthew sighed and continued walking over to her.

"Hey," Matthew said. "Is it okay if I join you?"

Victoria smiled.

"Of course," she said.

Matthew sat down on the sand.

"I brought you a drink," he said as he handed her the cup.

"Thank you," she said as she took a sip.

Matthew looked up toward the stars. They shined brightly through the dark sky. Several comets shot across the sky.

"It's beautiful," Victoria said.

Matthew turned to Victoria. He looked at the flower crown she had just put on her head.

"Yeah..." he said, "it is."

Matthew lay down on the sand.

"You know..." he started, "I didn't really want to say this since we're together under very bad circumstances, but... I've really enjoyed this. The time we've had together so far."

Victoria looked at Matthew. Her face was emotionless for a second, but then she smiled.

"So have I," she finally said.

Victoria yawned and lay down next to Matthew.

"I wish this night wouldn't end," she said.

"I know how you feel," Matthew said.

The stars drifted away as Matthew fell asleep.

• • •

Matthew woke up in the middle of the night. He was lying right next to Victoria, who was asleep with her hand over his chest. She looked so beautiful in the light of the stars.

"I think I do like you," Matthew whispered.

Chapter Seven:
The Maze

Matthew opened his eyes to see Kun-Alu staring at him, inches away from Matthew's face. Matthew gasped as he caught his hands on fire.

"I didn't mean to scare you," the king apologized. "I came to tell you that The Majesty is almost fully repaired."

Matthew stopped the fire. Victoria lightly stretched across the sand as she began to wake up.

"What time is it?" she asked.

"Your countdown says that you have thirty-nine hours remaining," Kun-Alu informed.

His mask tilted to the side.

"I would hurry if I was you. Rovunt is nearly a full day's travel away."

Victoria stood up on the sand and walked over to the jet.

"I'm going to go change," she said.

Matthew got up as well. He looked down at the grass skirt he was wearing.

"I should change too," he said. "Thanks for waking us up, Kun-Alu."

The king's mask rotated again.

"Of course, my friend," he said.

Matthew walked over to a small cave and opened the backpack he got from the Supplier. He pulled out a new set of underclothes, a black t-shirt, and some black jeans.

"Perfect," he said to himself.

A few minutes later he came out of the cave fully dressed in his black clothes and his green jacket, which was a bit torn up from the crash. Victoria was waiting for him outside. She was wearing her purple armor again, which was still badly damaged.

"How did you put on your armor so fast?" Matthew asked her.

Victoria drew Matthew's attention to her black belt, which had a large purple button in the center.

"The entire suit fits inside the belt," Victoria explained. "When I push this button, the metal pieces slide away in here, then come back out if I push it again." Matthew was impressed.

"I didn't know that," he said. "That suit is impressive."

Victoria smiled.

"Yeah, it is," she said.

Victoria was proud of her armor, just like she was proud of her jet.

"Hey, look at that," Matthew said.

Victoria looked over at the Majesty. Kun-Alu and a few dozen other people stood around the jet. Many of them held fruits and baskets in their hands. Matthew and Victoria walked over to the ship.

"What's all this?" Victoria asked.

"We have brought you some food for your journey," the king said. "We have fresh fruits and meat. You won't be going hungry anytime soon."

Victoria smiled.

"We appreciate your gifts, truly," she said.

The king's mask rotated sideways.

"It is our pleasure to serve you," he said.

Matthew smiled. Victoria opened up the side of the jet. Several villagers stepped inside and set down several boxes of food, plus a few spears.

"I've had a great time here," Matthew said to the Dowahns. "Thank you for your hospitality. I hope we can visit you again soon."

The people cheered. They'd love to have Matthew and Victoria back again.

"We need to go," Victoria said to Matthew.

Matthew entered the cockpit and strapped himself in.

"Are you ready?" Victoria asked.

"I think so," Matthew said.

Victoria started the jet. Everything seemed to be running smoothly. She lifted the jet off the ground.

"Everything's working so far," she said.

Matthew waved to the Dowahns that stood on the beach.

"Goodbye, Dowah," he said.

Victoria slowly brought the jet to the sky. She had to be sure that every crack had been fixed. If not, the jet would be destroyed, and they would be sucked into space. Victoria stopped the jet in space as she pressed several buttons on the dashboard.

"Everything seems to be working perfectly," she said as she held on to the yoke of the jet. "Are you ready?"

Matthew nodded as he looked out toward space.

"I'm ready," he answered.

Victoria started the jet at full speed. Matthew watched the stars pass by as they rocketed toward Rovunt.

• • •

Twenty-two long hours had passed, but Rovunt was nowhere to be seen. Matthew had eaten and slept twice, but Victoria hadn't slept a bit. She said that she was scared that they would be ambushed again. Matthew noticed that Victoria kept checking the countdown. He could tell that she was getting really worried.

"It's okay," he said to her. "We'll make it before the countdown ends."

Victoria nodded, but she ignored Matthew's statement.

"We should have been there by now," she answered quietly.

Matthew looked out of the windshield.

"Where are we?" he asked her.

"We're in empty space," she said, "just like I told you about before. There are no stars or planets out here, so there's no light. There's only... space. We have a saying on Valor. 'May the stars burn brightly for you tonight.' It's basically our way of saying 'Have a good and safe night,' but here in this void, nothing burns bright."

Matthew shuddered as he looked outside. It was pitch black here. The only lights that shone were the lights on the inside of the jet.

"This feels really strange," Matthew said.

He was literally staring into a dark void of nothing.

"Wait... what's that?" Matthew asked.

A tiny speck of light could be seen in the distance.

“I think it’s Rovunt’s sun,” Victoria said. “We must be getting close.”

Another hour of flying led Victoria to Rovunt, where it was fairly bright due to the one nearby sun. Victoria flew the jet down to the surface of Rovunt. The planet was mountainous and rocky, and hundreds of large boulders floated up in the sky. Victoria had to swerve to dodge a few small ones.

“What’s happening?” Matthew asked.

“There’s barely any gravity here,” Victoria said. “Everything is just floating around.”

Victoria activated a laser canon on the ship. The lasers hit a large boulder, which was crushed into smaller rocks.

“We’re almost at the surface,” Victoria said.

After a few more minutes of flying, Victoria set the Majesty down on an open plain. She pressed a few buttons on the ship, which locked it to the ground. Victoria’s hair began to lift up into the air.

“The Majesty won’t fly away,” she said, “but we might. Let me see if I have something for you.”

Victoria unlatched her seatbelt and floated over to the back of the jet. She came back a moment later with a white spacesuit. It included a helmet and a pair of thick boots.

“There’s no oxygen out on the surface,” Victoria said, “so you’ll need this.”

Matthew put the suit on and began to walk around the interior of the Majesty.

“The boots are weighted so that you’ll stay on the ground,” Victoria explained. “The boots on my armor will keep me down as well.”

Matthew took another few steps.

"It's perfect," he said.

Victoria's boots locked onto the floor of the Majesty as she walked over to the side door.

"Are you ready?" she asked with a smirk.

Matthew nodded. Victoria's helmet covered her head as she opened the side door, which sucked out all the oxygen in the cabin. Matthew was thrown out of The Majesty and into the dead space of Rovunt. Matthew shouted as he slowly fell to the ground. Victoria chuckled.

"Sorry," she apologized, "I had to do that."

Matthew chuckled nervously.

"It's okay," he said. "I should've seen that coming." Matthew tried to take a few steps, but he tripped and slowly fell to the ground.

"This is harder than it looks," he admitted.

Victoria extended her hand.

"Come on," she said, "I'll help you."

Matthew smiled as he took her hand.

"Let's go find the temple," Matthew said.

• • •

After a few long minutes of walking, Matthew began to get the hang of the suit. Matthew had to move his legs in a certain pattern to keep his balance. He tried walking by himself as Victoria looked at the map. The little image of Rovunt had a picture of a large temple that sat between two large mountains. One of the mountains had a small river that ran away from it. Victoria noticed a dried-up river bed on her left. A large rock sat halfway into the ground. A big dent and streak in the sand sat to the left of the boulder.

"The river flowed this way," Victoria said through her helmet, "so we should go in the opposite direction."

Matthew followed Victoria through the rocky landscape until they reached one of the large mountains.

"We're almost there," Victoria said.

"Let's keep moving," Matthew replied, "we're running out of time."

They kept on until they found the temple. This temple looked like the Greek buildings that Matthew had seen in his schoolbooks. Tall white pillars held up the roof, while marble stairs led up to the main room. Several large bubbles of glowing red liquid floated around in the area, creating a dome around the temple.

"What is this?" Matthew asked.

Victoria grabbed a stick and poked one of the bubbles with it. The stick burst into flames for a second before the lack of oxygen extinguished it.

"It's... lava," she said.

Matthew watched the bubbles pass by in front of him.

"Is that even possible?" he asked.

Victoria shook her head.

"It shouldn't be," she answered. "How are we going to get through?"

Matthew lifted his hand. He focused on the bubbles, which began to move as he moved his hand. Matthew lifted his other hand and moved them away from each other. The bubbles in front of him also moved away from each other, creating a path free of lava.

"After you," Matthew said.

Victoria walked through the path and looked around at the ground.

"There's no fire beast carved here," she said. "I think I can enter the temple."

Matthew and Victoria slowly walked up the long steps to the temple. A tall statue of a flaming phoenix stood inside the main room.

"Are you sure you want to risk it?" Matthew asked.

Victoria nodded.

"I'm sure," she said.

She took a step inside the temple. Nothing happened. Matthew entered the temple. The statue of the phoenix was plated with gold, and so were a few of the walls.

"Look at that," Matthew said as he pointed to a large pedestal in the center of the room.

A large key sat on the pedestal. The key was plain and black, but it looked ancient.

"I think that's the key," Matthew said as he stepped up to the pedestal.

"Be careful," Victoria warned.

Matthew reached out and grabbed the key. All was silent for a moment. Matthew felt a sudden pull to the ground as the gravity returned to normal.

"Not again..." he said as the ground started to crack.

The floor broke away as Matthew and Victoria screamed and fell to the bottom of the temple. Matthew hit a large rock on his way down, sending him through a different tunnel than Victoria. Matthew hit the ground hard. The floor was covered in sand. Matthew slowly stood up.

"Victoria!" he called.

There was no answer. Matthew stood up and placed the key in a pocket on his spacesuit. A light on his left gauntlet indicated that there was oxygen in the room. Matthew pressed a button on the side of his neck, which deactivated his helmet.

"Where am I now?" Matthew asked himself as he looked around the room.

Tall sandstone walls stood next to Matthew. The walls stretched in both directions before reaching an intersection at the end of the hallway. In the other direction, the walls created a dead end. Matthew found a picture on the wall, so he put his hand on it. The pictures began to move as a man tried to escape a large maze, which held many traps for him. There were flaming arrows, a giant boulder and even living skeletons that eventually threw themselves on top of him. Matthew looked down the hallway.

"It's a maze," he said to himself.

• • •

Victoria stood up and looked around the maze.

"Matthew!" she called.

There was no answer. Victoria looked at the wall next to her. It showed a giant boulder chasing a man. Victoria heard a deep rumble behind her.

"Perfect," she sighed.

Victoria used her rocket boots to fly over the boulder, which passed by under her. Victoria tried to fly high up into the room so that she could try to find Matthew, but a field of energy electrocuted her, throwing her back to the ground. She couldn't fly out. Victoria looked down the hallway, but she decided to walk in the opposite direction of the boulder. A skeleton sat halfway in the sand. Several of its bones had been crushed.

"You weren't so lucky," Victoria said as she stepped over it.

• • •

Matthew continued to cautiously walk down the hallway. He made a left turn, then a right. He eventually found that he was back in the hallway with the pictures on the wall. There was even a mark in the sand where he had fallen. Matthew cried out in anger as he banged his fist on the wall. The wall began to move as it opened a door to a second hallway. This hallway had no pictures on the wall, but the ground was made of stone. Matthew took a step inside. He started walking through the hall until he stepped on a stone tile that sunk into the floor with the weight of Matthew's heavy boots.

"Uh-oh," Matthew said.

He moved out of the way just before a large axe flew across the room and hit the wall behind him. Matthew walked over to the wall and pulled out the axe. A skeleton hung on the wall with an arrow stabbed through its head. Matthew sighed worriedly. He would need to be more careful.

• • •

Victoria found a hallway that was filled with a putrid smell. Victoria covered her nose.

"Disgusting," she said as she walked in.

This hallway was dark and damp. The light began to fade as Victoria moved further into the hall. Victoria pressed a button on her gauntlet, which turned on a few lights on the shoulders of her armor. Victoria heard a hissing sound nearby. She turned around just as a giant snake lunged toward her. She grabbed the snake's open jaws with her armored hands. She shut the snake's mouth and activated a long knife on the top of her right gauntlet, which she used to stab the snake in the head. The giant serpent went limp. Victoria pulled out the knife and dropped the snake to the ground. She continued walking until she found a door, which she tried to open. The door wouldn't even move, but Victoria was sure that she could escape through it. Victoria heard another noise in the darkness. Something was walking toward her. Victoria lifted her right gauntlet and activated the knife, the blade still wet with snake blood.

• • •

Matthew watched as a giant boulder rolled across the hallway right in front of him.

"Woah..." he said to himself.

He looked both left and right. Nobody was in sight. Matthew decided that the boulder was probably meant to keep people away from something, so he walked in the direction it came from. He took a few wrong turns, but he eventually found himself near a dark hallway with a terrible smell.

“What died in here?” Matthew whispered to himself.

He took a few steps inside before he heard a noise. Matthew raised his axe. Something was lurking in the shadows. Matthew heard another noise, like a knife being pulled out of its sheath. Startled, he immediately jumped out and attacked whatever stood in the darkness. Victoria jumped out of the darkness with her knife raised. Reacting to the axe, she lifted her gauntlet knife to block the hit. Victoria struggled to block the force of the hit. Matthew was already very strong. Victoria could see that he was scared. Scared for his life. This mission had been dangerous. Matthew looked into Victoria’s eyes. At first, she looked angry, ready to fight for her life. Then she looked afraid, maybe afraid that she could have killed Matthew.

“I am so sorry...” Matthew said slowly as he dropped the axe. “I didn’t know it was you.”

Victoria put her knife away.

“It’s fine,” she said. “I didn’t know either. I thought you were another snake.”

Matthew looked at Victoria.

“Snake?” he asked.

Victoria lifted the snake she had killed.

“Woah...” Matthew said.

Victoria dropped the dead snake.

“Come look at this.”

Victoria showed Matthew the locked door at the end of the hallway.

“Do you still have the key?” she asked him.

Matthew pulled it out of his pocket. He inserted the key into the lock. It turned perfectly. Matthew slowly pushed open the door. The room was dark, but the walls glowed red with heat.

Lava flowed around the edges of the room. In the center of the room stood another tall pedestal, which held another key.

"That must be the key to the Fire Temple," Victoria said. "The other key only opened this door."

Matthew walked over to the pedestal. The large black key held a small gem on the bottom, which was red and transparent.

"This is it," Matthew said as he reached for the key, "get ready to run."

Matthew lifted the key from the pedestal. A large red fog flowed out of the pedestal. The fog left the room and found the skeletons of the men who had died across the maze. The fog entered the skeletons and used them as bodies. The skeletons shrieked as they walked over to Matthew and Victoria. Matthew could hear the screeching in the distance.

"What just happened?" he asked.

Victoria activated her helmet.

"Let's hope we don't find out," she said.

• • •

Matthew and Victoria ran through a long hallway. Several skeletons followed closely behind them. Matthew took off his boots as he ran and threw them at the skeletons.

"What are you doing?!" Victoria shouted.

"They're too heavy," Matthew answered. "The skeletons are going to catch up to me."

Victoria and Matthew continued running down the hallway. They stopped when they found the spot where Matthew entered the maze.

"This is pointless," Matthew said. "How are we going to get out of here?"

Victoria looked around the maze.

"I don't know," she said. "Maybe we could..."

Victoria stopped as she looked at the key in Matthew's hand. The transparent gem revealed a tiny sliver of white on the sandy floor.

"Matthew," Victoria said, "look through the gem in the key."

Matthew held the key up to his eye. Everything appeared red except for several white arrows that had been painted onto the walls of the maze. The arrows, which could only be seen through the gem of the key, pointed to the right.

"Woah!" Matthew said. "There are arrows on the walls. Let's go this way."

Matthew ran with the key up to his eye. The arrows directed him through a hallway that shot flaming arrows at them. Matthew and Victoria didn't stop running. Instead, they picked up the pace.

"Keep going!" Matthew said.

They ran until they met a group of seven skeletons, which Victoria attacked head-on. She used her suit to punch and kick the skeletons, destroying them. She smacked the head off of one skeleton, then grabbed the head of another and smashed it into a wall, crushing it to pieces. In ten seconds, the skeletons were dead.

"Don't stop!" Victoria said.

The bones on the ground began to shake as the fog rebuilt the skeletons. Matthew continued running. He followed the arrows on the wall until they led him to a dead end.

"This is it," Matthew said.

He put the key in his pocket and began to touch the wall.

"There has to be a button or something..." he said.

Victoria started looking for an opening of some kind, but she found nothing. A few skeletons found Matthew and began to attack. Matthew lifted his axe and crushed the head of a skeleton.

"I don't understand," he said. "The exit should be right here!"

Victoria killed a skeleton by beating it with its own arm.

"Wait..." Victoria said, "do you hear that?"

A rumble could be heard nearby. The noise quickly grew as the giant boulder came crashing toward them.

"Move!" Victoria said as she flew away.

Matthew jumped to the side. The skeletons were crushed as the boulder ran them over and crashed through the empty wall, which opened to the outside. The boulder began to float away as the gravity disappeared. Matthew and Victoria also began to float. All the air inside the maze began to escape through the broken wall. Large gusts of wind lifted the loose sand from the ground, blowing dust everywhere. Matthew held on to the wall of the maze as he reactivated his helmet.

"No..." he said to himself.

The force of the air pulled Matthew out of the temple and toward the dome of lava. Victoria flew over and grabbed Matthew's hand just before he hit the lava. Matthew was breathing heavily.

"Thank you," he said.

"Of course," Victoria said, "now let's get out of here."

Matthew created another gap through the dome, which they escaped through.

"That wasn't so bad," Victoria said tiredly.

Matthew looked back at the temple, which collapsed in on itself. The debris then began to float through the air.

"I guess not," Matthew said with a sigh.

Victoria and Matthew entered The Majesty. Matthew deactivated his helmet as he entered the cockpit.

"How much time do we have left?" he asked.

Victoria pulled up the countdown. She was silent for a minute.

"Twelve hours," she said. "It takes longer than that to get back to Valor."

Matthew looked down at the key in his hand.

"We have to try," he said. "We only have one temple left: the one on Lahtaris."

Victoria started the jet. She transferred all power to the engines. The Majesty shot forwards through space toward Lahtaris. The stars passed by even faster than before. The jet was using its full power. A red light began to blink, which Victoria turned off. They were flying dangerously fast now. Matthew looked at Victoria. She was scared. A tear ran down her face.

"Hey," Matthew said to her.

Victoria looked at Matthew.

"We'll make it," he said. "I know we will."

Victoria nodded, but she said nothing. Matthew looked out toward space. They had to make it.

Chapter Eight: Wrath

Matthew quietly gasped as Lahtaris came into view of the Majesty. The fiery planet was black and rocky, but many parts of it glowed red from thousands of volcanoes and streams of lava. Large geysers of fire and a nearby red moon added to the apocalyptic red color. A nearby black hole had begun swallowing a glowing green planet. Matthew thought that Lahtaris was terrifying, but still beautiful in its own way.

"Is that a black hole?" Matthew asked, remembering what he and Victoria had been talking about earlier.

The hole itself was invisible, but Matthew could see the color of the green planet circling the area around it. Victoria nodded her head.

"Yes," she answered, "but don't worry about it. It's too far away to harm us."

Victoria sounded worried, but not about the black hole. Matthew knew that her hope for her father was growing smaller as time began to run out.

After another few minutes of flying, Victoria landed the Majesty on a strip of land away from any lava. Matthew exhaled nervously as he looked up at the red sky.

"We need to hurry," Victoria said as she checked the countdown. "We only have... two hours left."

Matthew nodded, but he said nothing. Victoria pressed a few buttons on her gauntlet, which copied and displayed a hologram of the two-hour countdown.

"We would need a miracle to make it back in time," she whispered.

Matthew and Victoria walked out of the jet and began running in the direction of the red moon.

"The moon should be aligned with the Fire Temple," Victoria explained as she checked the map.

Matthew could tell that Victoria was still worried. After all, it would be impossible to travel all the way back to Valor in two hours. She was right. They would need a miracle.

• • •

The temple was finally visible. Tall spires reached up toward the sky. The white walls appeared red from the moon, making the temple look like something out of a horror movie. The temple itself was enormous, large enough for a giant to live inside. A large moat of lava circled the temple.

"Hold on," Victoria said as she grabbed Matthew's hand.

Victoria used her jet boots to fly over the moat. Matthew ran to the tall doors of the temple, which reached at least one hundred feet up. The doors had large handles about halfway up, but the keyhole was enormous. Matthew looked at the small black key he held in his hand. There was no way it would fit inside the lock.

"Why don't you look through the gem again?" Victoria suggested.

Matthew held the red gem up to his eye. A small keyhole became visible on the door in front of him. He pushed the key in and tried turning it, but the key wouldn't move.

"Come on," he said worriedly as he heated his hands.

Matthew watched as the heat from his hands entered the key and flowed through the door, causing tiny dark cracks to glow red. Matthew felt that he now had a grip on the doors, so he twisted the key. The key turned and unlocked the door. Matthew lifted his hands and began to pull at two imaginary handles, which began to open the doors. Matthew shuddered when he saw the darkness inside the castle. Only a few red lights flickered here and there, lightly illuminating a large path.

"I saw something written on the walls of the temple on Exorda," Matthew started, "You and I both know what's in there, don't we?"

Victoria nodded. Her eyes began to fill with tears. Matthew turned to Victoria.

"In case I don't make it..." he began.

"Don't..." Victoria said sadly. "Don't say that."

Victoria wrapped Matthew in a tight hug.

"I'm scared," he said shakily.

"I know," Victoria said. "So am I. I've been scared for so, so, long, but... you gave me hope. Hope that Lord Vencrim really can be defeated."

Victoria let Matthew go.

"Even if you don't find the Fire Sword, I know you're worthy of being The Eternal Flame."

Matthew swallowed and nodded his head.

"Thank you..." Matthew said, "for believing in me."

Victoria nodded and smiled warmly as a tear fell from her eye. A loud booming noise thundered across the sky. Matthew and Victoria looked up and saw a Destroyer capsule entering the atmosphere.

"You go," Victoria said. "I've got this."

"Victoria... I..." Matthew started.

There was a moment of silence as he looked directly into her beautiful brown eyes, possibly for the last time.

"Just... be careful," he finished.

Victoria nodded her head.

"You too," Victoria said.

Matthew turned and walked into the temple. Victoria's helmet covered her head as she pulled out her retractable sword and extended the blade. The Destroyer capsule landed on the ground near the temple. The Destroyer climbed out and began to march toward Victoria, who used her boots to rocket toward the Destroyer. She yelled out as she lifted her sword to strike the giant robot as it lifted its arm to crush her.

• • •

The doors of the temple closed behind Matthew, covering him in darkness. Then, dozens of torches on the wall ignited, lighting up the room. A statue of a giant dragon sat in the middle of the room. The dragon stood at least fifty feet tall, and it had dozens of long sharp teeth. One of the dragon's claws was as big as Matthew's head. Matthew walked past the statue and began to look for The Fire Sword. He searched room after room, but he couldn't find it. One room was filled with an enormous pool of bubbling lava. Another room was filled with dozens of piles of bones. The doorway of each room was enormous, but Matthew already knew why.

"Whoo arre youu?" a rough voice asked.

The voice seemed to be coming from every direction.

"I am Matthew Benson, The Eternal Flame," Matthew answered bravely.

The voice growled.

"I was The Eternal Flame once," the voice said, "but I was... greedy. I wanted more power."

Matthew continued looking for the sword, but he still couldn't find it. The voice continued.

"Majesto told me I was powerful enough to stop Lord Vencrim and bring peace to the universe, but I didn't care. I didn't want to kill Lord Vencrim so that I could bring peace or eradicate evil. I wanted to kill him to prove that I was the most powerful being in the universe."

Matthew opened two large doors made of solid gold and stepped inside the room. He had to shield his eyes from the bright lights inside. Thousands of golden objects were piled high inside the room. At the end of the room sat a sword that was stabbed into a pile of gold coins. The sword had a black handle with a gold cross guard and pommel. The cross guard had a red gem embedded into it. Matthew gazed at the majestic sword in awe. He had finally found it.

"Majesto then told me that I had become unworthy of being The Eternal Flame," the voice said. "Majesto trapped me here so that I could never escape. And just to mock me, he hid the Fire Sword here with all my other treasures. Right in my grasp, yet so far away."

Matthew began to walk toward the sword.

"I have been trapped in here ever since, but you were foolish enough to release me."

Matthew stopped walking. In the main room of the temple, the statue of the dragon began to shake. The eyes of the statue glowed red as the pieces of stone began to fall away, revealing a giant red dragon. The dragon's roar could be heard throughout the hallways and even outside of the temple.

"I am Wrath, The Eternal Flame!" the dragon shouted.

• • •

Victoria fell to the ground. The Destroyer had knocked her down with its flying hand. The robot was missing its left arm, but it was still a worthy opponent. Another boom was heard in the sky. Another Destroyer was coming. Victoria flew toward the robot and tried to cut off its leg, but the robot stepped to the side and grabbed her as she passed. The robot then smashed Victoria into the ground, breaking the right side of her helmet. The robot tried to punch her into the ground, but Victoria rolled over and dodged it. She then tried to cut off the robot's hand, but her sword was no longer strong enough. The robot used its laser to blast Victoria. She lifted the sword to protect herself, but the blade broke in her hand. Victoria threw the useless handle to the ground. The second Destroyer capsule crashed behind Victoria. Its giant hand reached out to grab her. Victoria fell as she moved to avoid it. The second Destroyer climbed out of its capsule. Both Destroyers activated their lasers, which Victoria struggled to avoid. Victoria glanced at the Fire Temple. Large storm clouds had begun to swirl around above it, occasionally striking the towers with fiery red lightning.

"Please hurry, Matthew," she said.

• • •

Wrath flew into the treasure room. He looked around at all of his possessions. The Fire Sword was still in its usual place on top of the tallest pile of gold.

"Wherrre arre youu?" he growled.

The giant dragon took another step into the room, which shook the whole floor. Matthew hid behind a small pile of gold. He glanced at Wrath, who was sniffing a pile of colorful gems.

"You can't hide forever," Wrath said.

Matthew slowly started making his way toward the Fire Sword. Wrath sniffed around until he found a pile of gold. Wrath roared as he slashed his claws at the pile. Nobody was there.

"You are just a child," the dragon sneered. "You are not worthy of my sword."

Matthew sighed quietly.

"I know I'm not worthy," Matthew said.

Wrath couldn't tell where Matthew's voice was coming from.

"I've been a nobody my entire life," Matthew continued. "People looked at me on the streets and felt sorry for me. My own parents didn't even want me."

Wrath roared as he swatted at another pile of gold.

"I've always looked at the world and I've hated it for what it was. A place of violence and hatred. Earth didn't accept me, but

Valor did. I don't know if Earth is beyond saving, but Valor isn't."

Wrath continued to search the room for Matthew.

"For some great and strange reason, I've been chosen to become The Eternal Flame," Matthew said. "The people of Valor are counting on me to protect them, and I won't let them down. I will take this sword and defend the people I've chosen to call my own, even if it costs me my own life."

The gem of the Fire Sword began to glow as Matthew approached it.

"You will die here!" Wrath roared.

He spotted a coin falling from a pile of gold. Wrath swatted the pile, revealing Matthew hidden behind it. Matthew ran toward the sword, but Wrath backhanded him into a pile of silver. Matthew coughed as he stood to his knees. He noticed a silver shield laying on the pile next to him.

"Foolish child," Wrath said as his throat began to glow.

The dragon roared and blew a large stream of fire at Matthew, who lifted the silver shield to block the flames. The fire was hot, even for Matthew. He noticed that his skin began to blister. Matthew winced as he slowly began to sidestep toward the Fire Sword. Wrath realized that Matthew was getting closer to the sword, so he stopped breathing fire.

"You cannot win," Wrath said.

Matthew was in pain. His arms were burned by Wrath's fire. The silver shield sizzled from the flames. Matthew saw that Wrath's throat began to glow red again. Matthew had an idea.

"Give me your best shot," Matthew said with a smile.

Wrath opened his mouth to breathe fire as Matthew spun around as hard as he could, throwing the shield at Wrath. The shield flew through the air like a frisbee. Matthew created a fireball as hot as he could and threw it at the shield, pushing it directly toward Wrath. Wrath roared as the hot shield flew straight into his mouth, cutting his throat and choking him. He coughed and sputtered as he spit out the burning shield. Wrath smashed the ground where Matthew had stood, but Matthew was no longer there.

"You will die for that!" Wrath roared.

"I don't think so," Matthew said as he reached for the Fire Sword.

Wrath roared as he blew a gigantic flame toward Matthew, who barely managed to grab The Fire Sword. Matthew lifted the sword and used it to block the fire. He took a step forward as the sword continued to work like a shield, repelling the fire. The blade of the Fire Sword burst into flames as it began to give Matthew more power. Matthew could feel himself getting stronger. Out of breath, Wrath stopped blowing fire.

"My turn," Matthew growled.

Matthew roared and breathed a huge stream of fire at Wrath, who backed away in pain. Matthew continued to walk forwards. His eyes turned a glowing red color as he picked up the silver shield. Wrath began to flap his huge wings and fly up into the air.

"Impossible!" Wrath growled. "I am all-powerful!"

Matthew raised his sword and shield.

"Not anymore," Matthew said. "Majesto was right. You're not worthy of this power."

Wrath roared and flew at Matthew with rage as he swung his huge claws at him. Matthew used the shield to block the hit, then he pushed the sword through Wrath's chest, stabbing him. A huge wave of fire erupted from the sword, pushing itself into Wrath's body. Wrath shrieked as his body began to fade into ashes.

"Nooo!" he shouted.

Wrath fell to the ground as he slowly faded away. He swiped his claw at Matthew, who blocked the hit with the shield. Matthew then swung his flaming sword at Wrath's arm, cutting it off. Wrath shrieked as his entire arm immediately faded away. Soon there was nothing left of the giant dragon but a large pile of dust. Matthew dropped the shield and looked down at the Fire Sword. The glowing red gem seemed to be looking directly at Matthew, who felt that the sword somehow wanted him to have it.

"Thank you," Matthew said hesitantly.

Could the Fire Sword understand him? The red gem flickered. Matthew smiled.

"Now let's go help Victoria."

• • •

Outside of the temple, Victoria fought the giant Destroyers. She was sweating from the heat of the planet. The armor that usually kept her cool now felt like an oven. The robots had managed to damage her armor and her rocket boots, which no longer worked. Her suit felt heavier since it had lost power, making it harder to fight. Victoria's face was cut up on the right side. Blood dripped from above her eye. Her arms and legs were tired. She was reaching her limit. The robots were still in relatively good shape. One was missing both arms, and the other was missing an eye. Both were still fully capable of destroying Victoria in an instant. The Destroyer without arms stepped on Victoria, pushing her into the ground. Victoria groaned under the pressure. Her armor barely held up. The Destroyer lifted its leg again. Victoria tried to activate the Disabler, but she dropped it as the Destroyer stomped on her again. She knew she couldn't take another hit. Victoria closed her eyes. She could see the green fields of Valor. Her family stood there, waiting for her. The sound of metal clanged loudly through the air. Victoria opened her eyes. She watched as the armless Destroyer fell to the ground. Matthew had just jumped high through the air and thrust his sword into the Destroyer's chest, knocking it over. Matthew pulled the sword out of the Destroyer.

"Are you okay?" Matthew asked Victoria, who nodded slowly.

"I'm okay," she said, exhausted.

Matthew looked at the other Destroyer. The robot's eyes began to glow red. Matthew lifted the Fire Sword as his own eyes turned red. Beams of lasers shot out of Matthew's eyes, drilling holes through the Destroyer's head. The robot's head exploded as its body fell to the ground. Surprised, Matthew lowered his sword.

"You're more powerful than before," Victoria said as Matthew helped her to the ground.

He could see that she was in bad shape.

"Let's get you to the jet," he said worriedly.

• • •

Matthew and Victoria limped over to the Majesty.

"I'm out of power," Victoria said as she attached a cable from her armor to the ship's dashboard.

Victoria pulled up the countdown. She sighed.

"We have thirty minutes left," she said.

Matthew sunk down into the co-pilot seat.

"We couldn't have failed," he said.

A tear fell from Victoria's face.

"We failed," she said sadly.

Matthew looked up at the red sky in despair. They had lost. Everything that they had done over the past three days had been for nothing.

"Victoria, I..." Matthew started.

He paused as he noticed that something in the sky was different, but what was it? He studied the skies intently. That was it! The green planet from earlier was missing. He remembered the nearby black hole floating silently in space. Matthew had an idea. He began to press a few buttons on the dashboard.

"You said that Lord Vencrim created a wormhole near Valor, right? One that he could use to transport his ships?"

Victoria looked over at Matthew.

"Yeah..." she answered. "Why?"

Matthew pulled up a hologram of the wormhole and the black hole. They were perfectly lined up with each other through space. No planets stood between them.

"What if we use the black hole as a portal back to Valor?" Matthew asked.

Victoria shook her head.

"It's impossible," she answered. "Only Lord Vencrim's ships can withstand the wormhole, but I don't even know how. The gravity of a black hole is way too strong. Not even light can escape it. If we were to reach the end of the black hole, we would enter the wormhole, which would immediately collapse in on itself. We would be destroyed."

Matthew pointed at the hologram.

"The gravity of the black hole on this side would pull us in, right?" he asked Victoria.

"Yes," she answered, "and the other side would throw us out, but we'd be crushed before that happened."

Matthew thought for a few moments.

"Once we reach the middle," Matthew continued, "the hole will collapse, but if we had a ship with a very powerful energy shield, would it keep the wormhole from collapsing?"

Victoria nodded.

"I guess it could," she said, "but the Majesty's shields aren't that strong. The shields would need to have an energy source of infinite power, but nothing like that even exists."

Matthew lifted his sword.

"What about this?" he asked.

Victoria slowly grabbed the handle of The Fire Sword.

"You saw how strong it made me," Matthew continued. "I know it's more powerful than it looks. I can feel it."

Victoria attached a few cables to the sword. Victoria gasped as every light on the jet instantly lit up, as did Victoria's armor. They were both at full power.

"I think we have a chance," Matthew said.

Victoria looked up at the black hole. She was silent for a minute.

"If this doesn't work... we'll be killed," she finally said.

Matthew nodded.

"I'm willing to risk it if you are," he answered.

Victoria was silent for another minute. She looked over at the countdown. Time was almost up.

"Okay," she said. "Let's do it."

Chapter Nine: Return to Valor

Victoria pressed several buttons on the dashboard as she started up the Majesty. The black hole became visible as the windshield turned green.

"This is crazy," she said.

Matthew buckled his seatbelt.

"I know," he said, "but the last three days have been crazier."

Victoria's jet headed toward the black hole.

"Our mission was to find the Fire Sword and rescue your father," Matthew said to Victoria. "I told Wrath that I found purpose in protecting Valor. Honestly... I don't really care to live if I fail. Earth has nothing for me anyways."

Victoria gazed into the dark abyss of the black hole. The hole's force of gravity began to pull the Majesty toward itself.

"At least if I die..." Matthew continued, "I get to die with you."

Matthew turned to face Victoria. She looked at him with her gorgeous brown eyes. She was afraid, but Matthew's words calmed her. Matthew extended his hand toward Victoria.

"I've fought alongside the greatest warriors in the universe," Victoria said. "None of them were greater than you."

Victoria took Matthew's hand and held it tightly.

“When I tighten my grip, focus your powers to the sword,” Victoria said.

The jet began to shake as they were pulled into the black hole. The shaking intensified as the light began to fade. The force of gravity was almost too much for them to bear.

The noise inside the black hole was unexplainable. It was either negatively quiet, or insanely loud, echoing like a million toolboxes amplified through a billion speakers as The Majesty shook violently. Matthew couldn’t tell which it was.

“Hold on!” Matthew said.

His voice was shaking. It felt like every part of his body wanted to escape the black hole, but he felt completely powerless against it. It was like he wanted to laugh and cry, live and die at the same time. He couldn’t think. He could only feel the force of gravity on the Majesty. The darkness inside the black hole was even deeper than the darkness in space near Rovunt. Not a bit of light was perceivable, even the light from the dashboard of the jet.

“We’re almost halfway there!” Victoria shouted.

Matthew gripped his sword tightly. His body felt like it was going to fall apart.

“Now!” Victoria yelled as she tightened her grip on his hand.

Matthew focused his powers to the sword, which lit up in the darkness. The jet lurched forwards even faster as it entered the second hole’s opposite force of gravity. Matthew yelled as he held onto the sword. The ship kept picking up speed. A light was visible at the end of the hole.

“The shield is working,” Victoria shouted, “Let go of the sword when I tell you.”

A layer of red energy covered the Majesty as the walls of the tunnel began to collapse over the ship. Matthew felt the ship jolt as one of the back thrusters of the Majesty exploded, slowing them down. The ship struggled to push against the force of the collapsing tunnel.

"Come on..." Matthew said.

Several alarms began to blare as the Majesty began to creak and groan under the pressure of the tunnel.

"No..." Matthew whispered.

Victoria plugged her suit back into the control panel, giving the Majesty one last push of energy. The jet shot out of the wormhole just as it collapsed on itself. Free from the pressure of the tunnel, the Majesty returned to an incredible speed as it rocketed directly toward Valor.

"Let go!" Victoria yelled as she let go of Matthew's hand.

Matthew dropped the Fire Sword. The surface of Valor appeared directly in front of them as they stopped.

Victoria pulled on the yoke of the jet to avoid hitting a large mountain.

The second thruster of the jet exploded as the Majesty began to dive down.

"Hold on!" Victoria shouted.

The jet hit the ground and began to roll and flip over. After a few turns, the Majesty landed right side up, but nearly every part of it was destroyed.

"Are you okay?" Victoria asked.

Matthew crawled out of the broken windshield and fell out onto the ground. He bent down and vomited on the snowy ground. The speed had churned his stomach.

"I'm okay," he said weakly.

Everything felt like it was still vibrating. He tried to stand, but he couldn't. He couldn't hear anything, only a loud ringing and a faint whisper of Victoria's voice. Matthew laid down on the snow to rest for a minute.

"How much time do we have?" Matthew asked.

Victoria, also struggling to stand, stepped out of the Majesty. She activated the countdown on her gauntlet.

"Something must be wrong with my gauntlet," she said. "It says we have seventy-three hours left."

Matthew slowly sat up.

"Why does it say that?" he asked.

Victoria walked back over to the Majesty and turned on the main countdown. It also read seventy-three hours.

"It must be broken," she said.

Matthew heard a loud rumble nearby.

"Do you hear that?" he asked.

Victoria nodded. Her face suddenly filled with fear.

"Get down!" she said quietly.

Matthew quickly jumped over to the Majesty and crouched down underneath it with Victoria. A large black ship flew overhead. The ship was shaped like a triangle. Leveena's lightning jet screeched by after it.

"They're attacking the castle..." Victoria said.

"Again?" Matthew asked.

Matthew looked over at the castle, which was barely visible in the distance. The walls of the castle were perfectly intact.

"But the ships already destroyed that wall..." Matthew said. "Then Leveena broke down the door."

The triangular ship launched a missile at the castle, causing a large part of a tower to collapse. Dozens of bricks fell to the ground. Leveena's jet screeched by and destroyed the door with her jet.

"What's happening?" Matthew asked.

Victoria shook her head.

"I don't know," she said.

"How fast were we flying earlier?" he asked.

Victoria checked her gauntlet. She was silent for a moment.

"Faster than light," Victoria answered nervously.

Matthew looked over at the castle.

"Is it possible that we accidentally... traveled through time?"

Victoria looked at her gauntlet. It read the time and date that they left Valor.

"Lord Vencrim must've programmed the wormhole to eject his ships at this exact time and date," Victoria said, "but since we just flew through it at an impossible speed..."

Matthew sighed.

"We were ejected at the same time," he concluded as he sat back down in the snow.

"What do we do now?" Victoria sat down next to him.

"I don't know. But now I think we have enough time to make a good plan."

Matthew sighed as he looked back at the castle. This was too crazy. He had hoped that they could return to valor in thirty minutes. Now here they were three days before!

"What are we going to do?" he asked.

Victoria pulled her backpack out of the Majesty.

"We still have the Disabler," she said, "but that's pretty much it. Any ideas?"

Matthew looked at the round device. He lifted it up and compared it to the Fire Sword.

“I have half of an idea,” he said, “but for it to work... I’d have to actually beat Lord Leveena in a fight.”

Victoria nodded.

“Do you think I could do it?” Matthew asked.

“I know you can,” Victoria answered.

Matthew explained his full plan to Victoria. She thought it would work. The two waited under the Majesty until the original Majesty flew through the sky, away from Lord Leveena.

“There we are,” Matthew said as he watched the jet escape toward space.

Victoria looked at her gauntlet. After a few minutes, the countdown read exactly seventy-two hours.

“Leveena just accepted the deal,” Matthew said. “Are you ready?”

Victoria nodded.

“I’m ready,” she said. “Let’s go free my father.”

• • •

Victoria walked Matthew up to the broken doors of the castle. His arms were tied together with ropes. Two assassin robots stood guard at the doors.

“Tell Leveena that I brought her The Eternal Flame,” she said to the robots.

The robots said something in a low electronic language. The robots then stepped to the side, allowing Matthew and Victoria to enter the castle. Matthew held his breath as he walked past the tall robots. Another pair of robots escorted Matthew and Victoria to the throne room. Everything was working so far. Victoria entered the throne room with Matthew. Leveena sat on King Finnian's throne. She was more than shocked to see Victoria and Matthew.

"You... how is this possible?" she asked in confusion.

Victoria shook her head as she looked at Leveena with wide eyes.

"I don't know," she said.

Leveena's confusion disappeared as she looked back at Matthew.

"I see you've brought me something," Leveena said. "What happened to the Fire Sword? Did you change your mind?"

Victoria swallowed.

"Something like that," she answered. "Now, where's my father?"

Leveena snapped her metal fingers.

An assassin robot walked King Finnian into the throne room. The robot held a blaster to his head. The king was badly beaten.

"I made sure he was comfortable in his new cell," Leveena purred. "I think he liked it."

Victoria looked at Leveena.

"Let him go," Victoria said. "I'll give you the Fire Sword."

Leveena laughed.

"Is this a joke?" she asked. "You've only been gone for ten minutes."

Victoria pulled the Fire Sword out of the sheath on her belt. Leveena sat up straight on the throne.

"How did you find it so fast?" she asked in amazement.

"It doesn't matter," Victoria said. "Let my father go."

Leveena motioned with her hand for Victoria to come closer. Victoria brought the sword to Leveena. Victoria kept the sword face up as she walked. As she reached the throne, she bent down on one knee and presented the Fire Sword to Leveena.

"Please," Victoria cried, "let my father go, I'm begging you."

Leveena looked at the silver sword.

"My master will be very pleased with me," she said.

Matthew smiled.

"No, he won't," he said.

Leveena looked at Matthew, then back down at the sword. She turned it over to find the Disabler attached to the bottom. Leveena gasped. Several things happened at once. Victoria pressed a button on her gauntlet, which activated the Disabler, then she ran toward her father. Leveena cried out in pain as the Disabler sent millions of volts of electricity through her metal body, causing her to drop the sword. Matthew burned through the ropes on his wrists and ran toward Leveena. The assassin robot pointed the blaster away from Finnian and toward Victoria, which she had predicted it would. The assassin fired at her, but Victoria used her gauntlet knife to deflect the blast. Victoria lunged at the robot and stabbed her knife through its head. Matthew ran toward Leveena and picked up the Fire Sword. This was his chance to protect Valor.

"This is for King Finnian!" Matthew shouted.

He swung his sword with full force, slashing Leveena across the chest. Leveena fell off the throne and backed away. She stood up and swung her claws at Matthew, who backed away before he had been cut. The blade of The Fire Sword burst into flames as Matthew continued to fight Leveena. She screamed as she slashed at him, but she continued to miss. The Disabler had weakened her.

"This is for Valor!" Matthew yelled.

"No..." Leveena said quietly as Matthew cut her on her arm.

"And this is for Victoria!" Matthew roared as he swung his sword upwards, cutting part of Leveena's face.

He cut from the bottom of her lip up through her left eye. Leveena grabbed her eye as she fell to the ground. The purple light in her left eye was gone. Matthew's eyes began to glow red as he pointed his sword at Leveena. One more thrust of his sword would end her.

"Wait...!" she cried.

She lifted her hands to block the hit of the sword.

"Please..." she whispered.

Matthew stared into Leveena's eyes. She had no tears, but Matthew knew that she would have cried if she could have. She was truly afraid for her life. Matthew had killed Arach-Anach, and he had killed Wrath, but he just couldn't kill Leveena. She was too... human. The red lights in Matthew's eyes disappeared as he slowly lowered his sword. A giant hand suddenly punched through the wall, hitting Matthew. A Destroyer had smashed through the wall to save Leveena. Matthew hit the opposite wall and fell to the ground. Leveena stood up and ran toward the hole in the wall. She took one last sorrowful look at Matthew before she escaped. The Destroyer rocketed away, as did Leveena. The screeching sound of her jet could be heard in the distance. Matthew slowly stood up to his feet as Victoria ran over to him. His entire body hurt.

"Are you okay?" she asked worriedly.

Matthew nodded.

"I'm okay," he said with several coughs. "I just feel a little..."

The world turned black as Matthew fell back down to the ground. He could hear muffled voices around him. The last thing he heard was Victoria.

"Wake up, Matthew!" she cried. "Please..."

Chapter Ten: Victory

Matthew saw Lahtaris with all of its fire. He saw Rovunt, with its strange gravity. He also saw Dowah with its majestic beaches, and Exorda, the jungle planet. He saw Neon City on Zikanos with its bright city lights. Then Matthew saw Valor. The forest planet prospered as evil had finally been eradicated. Majestic horses and unicorns ran through grassy fields. Creatures that Matthew never knew existed, like Dwarves and Fairies, gathered together and sang songs. King Finnian's castle was fully restored as Matthew sat on the throne. There was finally peace on Valor.

Matthew opened his eyes. For a moment he believed that he was on his small bed back at the orphanage.

"What a dream..." he said to himself.

"I'm afraid not," Victoria said.

Matthew looked over at the chair next to his bed. Victoria sat there, patiently waiting for Matthew to wake up. Matthew realized that he was in some kind of medical room inside King Finnian's castle.

"What happened?" he asked as he sat up in his bed.

"You defeated Leveena. I saved my father..." Victoria answered. "We did it."

Matthew sighed in relief.

"I can't believe it," he said.

Victoria nodded.

"Neither can I," she said, "but Valor is safe now, thanks to you."

Matthew noticed the Fire Sword leaning against the wall next to his bed. He reached over and picked it up.

"We owe everything to this sword," Matthew said as he brushed his fingers over the gem.

The gem flickered.

"We owe everything to you," Victoria said. "Nobody has ever fought Lord Leveena and survived. You were very brave today."

Matthew smiled.

"I couldn't have done it without you," he said.

Victoria leaned in closer. Matthew closed his eyes as Victoria kissed him. Matthew felt like the world stopped for a moment. It felt like he had everything he ever wanted.

"Thank you, Matthew..." Victoria said quietly, "for everything."

King Finnian entered the room.

"Ah, you're awake!" he said.

Victoria quickly backed away from Matthew. Embarrassed, Matthew pretended to study his sword.

"Yeah," Matthew replied as he cleared his throat. "I'm awake."

The king walked over to Matthew's bed.

"My boy," Finnian said, "I must personally thank you for what you have done. You have saved my life and Victoria's. Valor will forever be in your debt."

The king shook Matthew's hand.

"I'm happy to serve you," Matthew said.

The king smiled.

"There will be a celebration tonight," he said. "We must formally thank you and Victoria for your heroics. We will have a great feast and we will laugh and jest merrily."

Matthew chuckled.

"I appreciate it, your Majesty." The king smiled.

"I will leave you to rest," The king said. "I will see you later tonight."

King Finnian left the room. Matthew turned to look at Victoria.

"So, uh..." Matthew started. "Are you excited for the party?"

Victoria smiled as she left the room.

"I'll see you later, Matthew," she said.

Matthew smiled as he laid back in bed.

The gem of the fire sword flickered.

"Yeah," Matthew said. "I like her too."

After a moment, Victoria walked back into the room.

"I almost forgot," she said, "I have a surprise for you. It's in there."

Victoria pointed to a tall cylinder-shaped object that was covered by a large sheet, then she left the room. Still in a bit of pain, Matthew slowly stood up and walked over to it. He pulled off the sheet, revealing a large display case. The Fire Sword flickered in approval.

"Woah..." Matthew said with a smile.

• • •

"We are here today to honor our greatest heroes," King Finnian said through a microphone. "Princess Victoria McCallaghan, please step forward."

Victoria smiled as she took a step toward Finnian. Victoria wore a long black cape with her purple armor, which had been fully restored. She wore red lipstick and let her jet-black hair fall to her back. Hundreds of villagers stood inside the ballroom of the castle to watch the ceremony. They cheered as Victoria stepped forward.

"You have shown great feats of bravery and courage," the king continued. "You fought until you faced death. For this, I present to you this medal."

Victoria lowered her head as King Finnian placed a gold medal around her neck. The medal had Valorian writing on it.

"Your heroism will be remembered in the history of Valor," the king finished. "Matthew Benson, Eternal Flame, please step forward."

Matthew smiled as he took a step forward. He wore a metal armor suit just like Victoria's, only it was bright red. He had a sheath with the Fire Sword on the left side of his black belt, and he wore a long black cape. Matthew's armor glistened in the light of the chandelier.

"You have shown great bravery and determination. You were courageous in the face of death, and you never ceased fighting for Valor, even against hopeless odds," the King said. "For this, I present to you this medal."

Matthew lowered his head to accept the medal, which was the same as Victoria's.

"Your heroism will be remembered in the history of Valor," King Finnian said.

Matthew took a step back so he could stand next to Victoria.

"Congratulations," she said with a smile.

"Thanks," Matthew said, "to you as well."

King Finnian continued speaking.

"On this day we shall forever remember Princess Victoria and The Eternal Flame, The Protectors of Valor!"

The crowd cheered as they bowed down on one knee to show respect for their new protectors.

"We're heroes now," Victoria said.

Matthew smiled. He had finally found his home.

• • •

Matthew stood on a balcony in the castle. He looked down at the village below. Snow was falling lightly as people cheered and danced on the roads. Bonfires were lit just to honor Matthew. People feasted in the castle and in the village. Valor was safe and well.

"How did you like your surprise?" Victoria asked.

She stood in the doorway of the balcony. Matthew looked down at his suit of armor.

"I love it," he answered. "Thank you."

Victoria nodded.

"Do you mind if I join you?" She asked.

Matthew smiled as he shook his head.

"Of course not," he said.

Victoria walked over to Matthew and stood next to him on the balcony. She looked out over Valor. From the balcony,

Matthew could see the ruins of the old city, the small village, and miles of dark forests.

"This is the kingdom we've been chosen to protect," she said.

"Yeah," Matthew said. "It's a great place."

Victoria looked sad for some reason.

"What is it?" Matthew asked her.

"I don't know," she answered. "I know we've had an incredible victory today but... I'm afraid it won't last."

Matthew gazed out into the distance.

"Yeah," he said. "So am I."

Victoria looked up at him.

"I'm still afraid of Lord Vencrim," Matthew answered. "I know he's still far more powerful than me, but... I have hope. I had a vision of Valor earlier today. Everything was perfect. Leveena and Vencrim were gone, and there was peace. True peace. It was the first positive vision I've had since I've gotten my powers. I think at the very least, we have a chance."

Victoria reached out and grabbed Matthew's hand.

"We'll train hard, Matthew. I'll teach you how to fight, then we'll stop him together," she said.

Victoria leaned her head on Matthew's shoulder.

"I know we will," Matthew sighed.

• • •

"You have failed me," Lord Vencrim growled.

"I'm sorry, Master," Lord Leveena responded, "I don't know what happened. I think they somehow used time travel. I was disconnected from..."

Lord Vencrim reached out his hand and began to choke Leveena using his powers. Leveena could feel her neck breaking and wires snapping as she was lifted off the ground.

"Don't give me excuses!" Lord Vencrim shouted.

He let go of Leveena's neck.

"You have served me well for nearly a decade," Lord Vencrim said calmly, "so I will give you mercy. Don't fail me again."

Leveena stood up to her feet.

"I won't, master," she said. "The next time I see The Eternal Flame, I will kill him."

Leveena marched out of the throne room. She walked over to her private room, where she had a charging station for her robot body. Leveena plugged her arm into a device as she began to recharge. A flying robot entered the room and began to repair the damage to her face and eye that Matthew had caused. Leveena pulled up a hologram of Matthew. She gazed longingly into his eyes. She remembered what had happened at the castle. He had spared her life. Nobody else had done that for her. Nobody else would. Lord Vencrim told her one thing, but her heart told her something else. Leveena threw the hologram at the wall as she screamed in conflict. She didn't know what she wanted anymore.

Epilogue

Ordinarily, books end with, 'THE END.' However, this is not the end. I have only told you a fraction of Matthew's story, which I suppose I could continue another time, should you be willing to hear it. I will tell you this though: Matthew may have been the first hero of his time, but he wasn't the last. Many more heroes rose up to defend the universe from evil, including myself. Back in my day, they called me The Mystery. How did I become a superhero? Well, that's a story for another time. As I write this, I know that the age of heroes is coming to an end. You may feel afraid sometimes, but that's okay. Just know this: as long as there is evil in this world, true heroes like The Eternal Flame will always rise up to meet it.

- Sincerely, Jonathan Everett Gold

About the Author

Israel Cazares II was born in the Imperial Valley. He created The Eternal Flame and the rest of his superhero world (Which he calls Mega Mysteries) when he was only nine years old.

Nowadays, Israel enjoys watching movies and posting reviews on his Instagram account, moviemaster_movie_reviews.

www.ingramcontent.com/pod-product-compliance
Lightning Source LLC
LaVergne TN
LVHW090611110826
845146LV00001B/341

* 9 7 9 8 2 1 8 2 4 0 6 7 7 *